Keep tears
My heart
For prose.

Train
Flammes bleues
Fleurs jaunes.
In the ditches
I am water.
Between
Grow kingcups of your childhood.
Sunk in my eyes
Skies of the churchyard.
Through arteries
Of gravel
Whispering to my grasses
The blood of goodbyes.
Flammes bleues
Fleurs jaunes
Their railways

ONCE IN EUROPA

TEXT: JOHN BERGER

PHOTOGRAPHS: PATRICIA MACDONALD

WITH ANGUS MACDONALD, PILOT

BLOOMSBURY

This story is dedicated to Jean-Paul

Published by Bloomsbury Publishing, New York and London.
Distributed to the trade by St. Martin's Press

A CIP catalogue record for this book is
available from the Library of Congress

ISBN 1 58234 070 6

Text first published in the USA in 1987 by Pantheon Books

This edition first published in Great Britain 1999
by Bloomsbury Publishing Plc

First U.S. Edition 2000
10 9 8 7 6 5 4 3 2 1

Origination by Radstock Reproductions Ltd, Bath, England
Printed in Hong Kong by C&C Offset Ltd

on to take her Baccalaureate.

Back of my arse! You see Odile as a schoolteacher?

She might be, said Mademoiselle Vincent.

No, no. She's too untidy. To be a teacher you have to be very tidy.

I'm not very tidy, said Mademoiselle Vincent, take me, I'm not very tidy.

You have a fine voice, Mademoiselle, when you sing, you make people happy. That makes up for a lot.

You're a flatterer, Monsieur Blanc.

She'll never be a teacher, Odile, she's too...he hesitated. She's too – too close to the ground.

Funny to think of those words now in the sky.

Twice in my life I've been homesick and both times it was in Cluses. The first time was the worst, for then I hadn't yet lived anything worse than homesickness. It's to do with life, homesickness, not death. In Cluses the first time I didn't yet know this difference.

The school was a building of five storeys. I wasn't used to staircases. I missed the smell of the cows, Papa raking out the fire, Maman emptying her pisspot, everyone in the family doing something different and everybody knowing where everybody else was. Emile playing with the radio and my screaming at him, I missed the wardrobe with my dresses all mixed up with Maman's, and the goat tapping with her horns against the door.

Ever since I could remember, everyone had always known who I was. They called me Odile or Blanc's Daughter or Achille's Last. If somebody did not know who I was, a single answer to a single question was enough for them to place me. Ah yes! Then you must be Régis's sister! In Cluses I was a stranger to everyone. My name was Blanc, which began with a B, and so I was near the top of the alphabetical list.

I was always among the first ten that had to stand up, or to file out.

In the school there I learnt how to look at words like something written on a blackboard. When a man swears, the words come out of his body like shit. As kids we talked like that all the time – except when we made traps with words. Adam and Eve and Pinchme went down to the river to bathe, Adam and Eve were drowned, who do you think was saved? At Cluses I learnt that words belonged to writing. We used them; yet they were never entirely ours.

One evening after the last lesson I went back into the classroom to fetch a book I'd forgotten. The French mistress was sitting at her table, her head buried in her hands, and she was crying. I didn't dare approach her. On the blackboard behind her, I remember it so well, was the conjugation of the verb *fuir*.

If somebody had asked me in 1952: What place makes you think of men most? I wouldn't have said the factory, I wouldn't have said the café opposite the church when there was a funeral, I wouldn't have said the autumn cattle market, I'd have said: the edge of a wood! Take all the edges of all the forests and copses in the valley and put them end to end like a screen, and there'd be a frieze of men! Some with guns, some with dogs, others with chain saws, a few with girls. I heard their voices from the road below. I looked at them, the slimness of the young ones, the way their checkered shirts hung loose, their boots, the way they wore their trousers, the bulges just below where their belts were fastened. I didn't notice their faces, I didn't bother to name them. If one of them noticed me, I'd be off. I didn't want to say a word and I didn't want to approach them. Watching was quite enough, and watching them, I knew how the world was made.

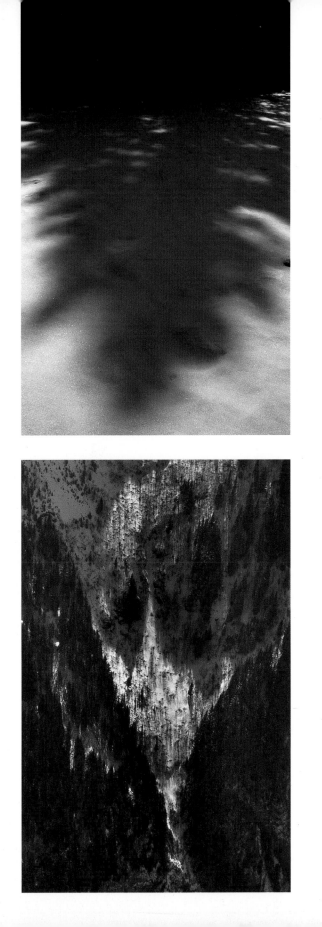

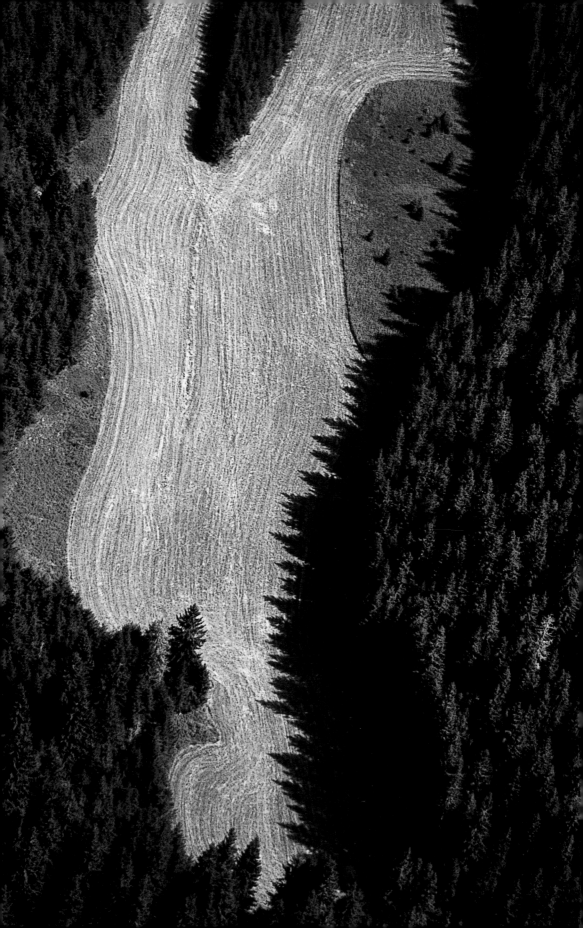

Take this loaf to Régis, said Mother. When it's freezing so hard the cold penetrates to your very bones and a man needs his food in such weather.

She handed me the bread. I ran as fast as I could towards the factory; there was ice everywhere and I had to pick my way. All was frozen – railway points, locks, window frames, ruts, the cliff face behind the factory was hung with icicles, only the river still moved. At the entrance I called to the first man I could see, he had blood-shot eyes and spoke with a strong Spanish accent.

Régis! Big man of honour! he shouted and jerked his thumb upwards. I waited there on the threshold for several minutes, stamping my feet to keep them warm. When Régis arrived he was with Michel. They were of the same class: '51. They had done their military service together.

You know Michel? asked Régis.

I knew Michel. Michel Labourier, nephew of the Marmot.

For God's sake come in and get warm, hissed Régis between his teeth as I handed him the loaf.

Father –

It's not the same if you're with me. Give me your hand. Jesus! you're cold! We've just tapped her.

They led me away from the big furnaces and the massive cranes overhead, which moved on rails in heaven, to another much smaller workshop.

You're going to school at Cluses? Michel asked me.

I nodded.

Do you like it?

I miss being at home.

At least you'll learn something there.

It's another world, I said.

Nonsense! It's the same bloody world. The difference is the kids who go to Cluses don't stay poor and dumb.

We're not dumb, I said.

He looked at me hard. Here, he said, take this to keep your brains warm. He gave me his woollen cap, red and black. I protested and he pulled the cap down on my head, laughing.

He's a communist, said Régis later.

At that time I didn't know what the word meant. We sat against a wall on a pile of sand. I let a handful of it run through my frozen fingers. I could feel its warmth through my stockings, touching my calves. Régis rummaged in a tin, took out his knife, and began cutting a sausage. There were some other men at the end of the shop.

So here's your sister come to see us! shouted one of them.

Odile's her name.

There's a Saint Odile, did you know that?

Yes, I shouted, her fête is the thirteenth of December.

She was born blind in Alsace, the man shouted back. He was at least fifty and thin as a goat's leg.

Was she?

She saw with her eyes for the first time when she was grown up. Then she founded a monastery.

The thin old man, who wasn't from the valley and who knew all about Saint Odile, was pulling on the chains of a pulley which worked a machine for grasping and lifting massive weights.

Now he's going to take the hat off the bread, said Régis.

I've just given you the bread, I said, understanding nothing.

See over there what's sizzling?

In the sand?

That's the bread with its hat on. Now watch!

Several men began to prod at the bread with long bars. To every blow the thing responded by spitting out fire. I was eating sausage. The old man's machine came down and lifted the top off the bread as if it were a cap. Under the cap everything was incandescent. I could feel the onrush of heat, although I was at the other end of the shop. The edges of the white-hot underneath were dribbling like a ripe cheese. When a dribble fell off and hit the ground it made a brittle noise like glass and turned black. All the men were holding up shields in front of their faces.

Each bread weighs a ton, said Régis. He drank from a bottle of wine and some of the wine ran down his neck. A ton, he continued, and ferromolybdenum is worth six thousand a kilo – work it out for yourself, you're still in school – one bread is sold for how much?

Six million.

Correct.

The bread, one and a half metres in diameter, was now phosphorescent in the sand. Régis wasn't looking any longer. I couldn't take my eyes off it.

Do you know the story of the Two Hunters? Régis asked.

Which story?

The story of the Two Hunters in the Forest.

The bread was changing colour. Its whiteness was turning violet. The violet of a child with croup.

I don't think I know the story of the Two Hunters.

Once there were two hunters in the forest up at Peniel: Jean-Paul and Jean-Marc.

Water from a pipe in the roof, with hundreds of holes in it, was falling like rain onto the bread. It was scarlet now.

Jean-Paul stops and says: Look over there, Jean-Marc! I can't see anything, replies Jean-Marc. Jean-Paul, still pointing, says: You must be blind, over there by the spruce, the one that's been uprooted. I can see the root and the earth and the stones, Jean-Paul, I can't see more.

The rain falling on the bread was making steam and it was hissing like a cricket.

The two hunters go deeper into the forest. Can you see her now? shouts Jean-Paul. Where? By the snow under the roots, Jean-Marc. In God's name, yes! screams Jean-Marc. Both men stop in their tracks, then they start making their way towards the tree. The snow is up to their waists. After a while they stop to get their breath back.

The bread was getting darker and darker in colour and I could scarcely see it anymore because of the clouds of steam coming off it.

Alive? asks Jean-Marc. Jean-Paul pushes his way forward. I can feel it from here! he cries. Be careful, Jean-Paul! Careful, Jean-Paul! Jean-Paul disappears. After a moment Jean-Marc hears his friend laughing, then his laugh changes into a sigh. The happiest sigh in the world, my friend. Jean-Marc knows what is happening so he looks at the tree tops. Whilst he looks at the tree tops, he counts. When he's counted to five thousand, he looks down, towards the spruce. No sign of Jean-Paul. Now it's Jean-Marc's turn.

The rain on the bread had stopped.

Jean-Marc too can feel it. He can hear the dripping. Like Jean-

Paul, he falls forward onto his face and starts to laugh. His laugh too becomes a sigh.

The bread was black now, with colours in it like oil.

Do you know what they were doing, Jean-Paul and Jean-Marc?

I shook my head.

You don't know, Odile, what the two hunters were doing?

No.

They were doing the lying-down waltz!

I looked at Régis and I thought: My kid brother – he was nine years older than I – you're drinking too much.

The sheet sail and everything hanging from it is turning south, towards the sun in a sky of the deepest winter blue, like the blue we had to wash clothes with.

On the day when Christ ascended to heaven, the Brass Band went from hamlet to hamlet in the village playing music. Their uniforms were newly pressed, their instruments were glittering in the sun, and the leaves of the beech trees were fresh as lettuces. They played so loud they made the windows rattle and tiles fall off the roof. And after each concert in each hamlet the public offered them gn¬le and cakes, so that by the end of the afternoon on Ascension Day, after a number of little concerts, the first and second saxophones were drunk as well as several trombones and a drum or two. On Ascension night, Father came home with his trumpet a little bit the worse for wear. With Father, though, nobody could tell till the evening. He never let it influence his fingers when playing.

He died on February the ninth, 1953. The next Ascension Day the band came to play in our orchard in his honour. They played a march from Verdi's *Aïda* and a tune called "Amazing Grace". Men from the factory lined the fence of the orchard listening to the music. Mother stood by the stable doors, arms folded across her bosom, looking up at the sky. And suddenly Papa's house with its three rooms, its hayloft, its little wooden balcony, its chopped wood, dwarfed the factory which was the size of six cathedrals.

"Amazing Grace" begins sad and gradually the sadness becomes a chorus and so is no longer sad but defiant. For a while I believed he was there. Later the music listens to itself and discovers that something has fallen silent. Irretrievably. He had left.

41

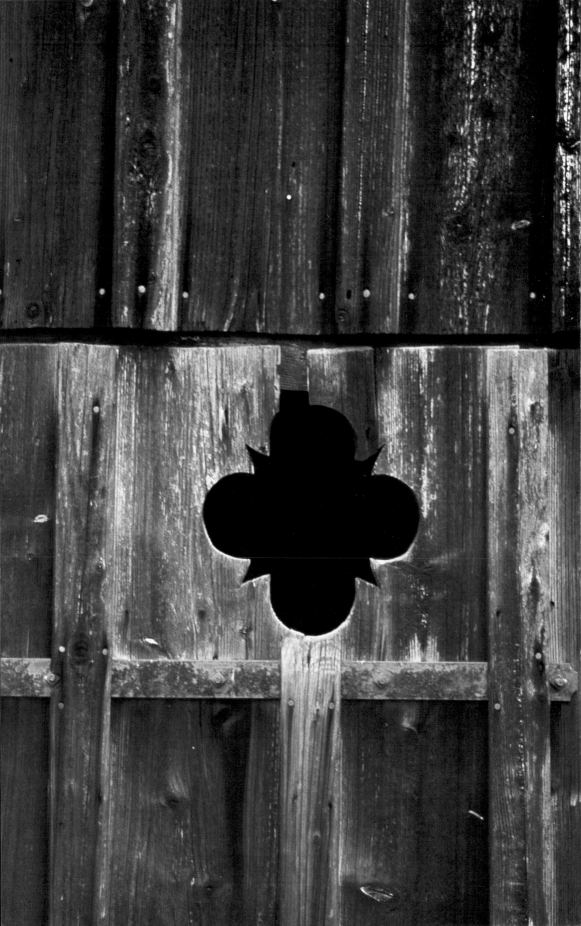

Whilst I was listening to "Amazing Grace" on that afternoon in May 1953, I touched something which I wouldn't be able to name until twenty years later. I touched the truth that the virility which women look for in men is often sly, slippery, impudent. It's not grand, what they're looking for. It's cautious and cunning, just like Father was.

The men on the other side of the fence started to clap and Michel waved at me. I turned away, saying to myself that only a communist would wave at a moment like that!

Michel's motorbike was red and was made in Czechoslovakia. The spare parts for it were cheaper than for any other bike, Michel said, because Czechoslovakia was communist and the communists didn't put profit before everything else. On several Sundays he asked me if I'd like to go for a spin with him and each time I refused. He was too sure of himself, he thought he knew better than anybody else in the valley. He had called my father a Chopping Block. Not to me. I heard about it from a friend. Achille Blanc has been a chopping block for others all his life! Those were his words. So I said no to him.

The sixth time he asked me was in August. We were both on holiday. The hay was in the barn. Régis had bought an old third-hand Peugeot and was painting it in the orchard. Emile was there in the house when Michel came. He drives well, Odile, said Emile, you've nothing to be frightened about. On Wednesday morning early, Michel announced, I'll pick you up at five. At five! I protested. Five's not too early if we're going to Italy! Italy! I screamed. Yet, however loud I screamed it, the word was having its effect. If we were really going to drive to Italy, everything was beyond my control. I said nothing more. And on Tuesday night I prepared my trousers, my boots, and a haversack with a picnic for us both.

45

We went over the Grand St. Bernard a little to the east of the Mont Blanc where the wind now is blowing the snow like my chiffon scarf against the blue sky. Neither of us knew what life had in store. Nothing happened. Michel had brought a thermos of coffee which we drank from for the first time near Chamonix. We passed a factory which, Michel said, was like a copy of ours. It took up less space. On the bike we climbed higher and higher. We ate our picnic above the tree line. I never breathed so much air in my life. Mouth, nose, ears and eyes all took in air. At the summit we threw snowballs at each other and saw the dogs. They were as big as ponies. There was a lake. A lake at that height was as surprising as tears at a victory.

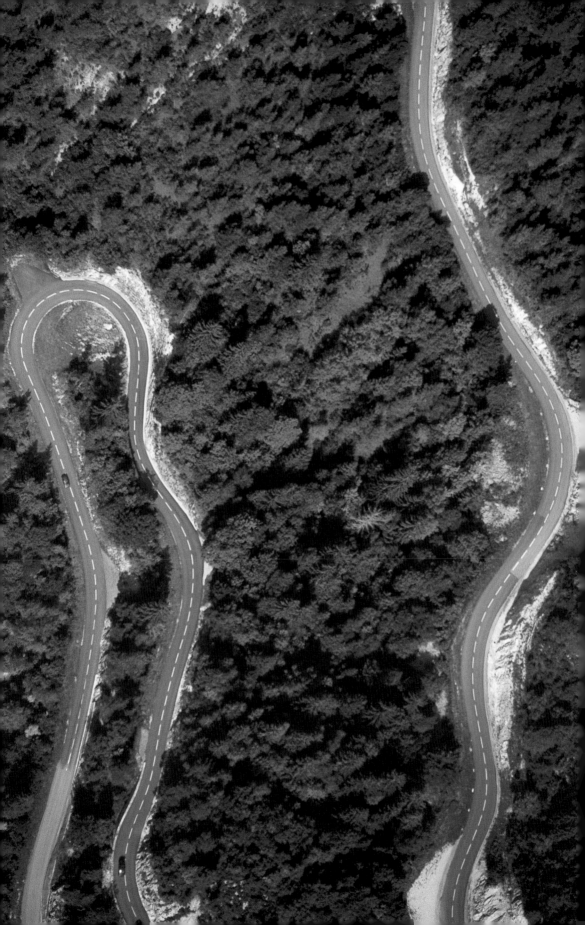

When the wind was too cold I put my head down against his leather jacket. I tucked my knees under his legs and held on with one hand to his leather belt. Around the hairpins I lay down with the bike like grass blown by the wind.

She overheated a bit on the last stretch, he said. You probably smelt the burnt oil?

Motor oil, I said, I don't know what it smells like.

On the red 350cc two-stroke twin motorbike made in Czechoslovakia we came down into Italy, on the other side of the mountain. The cows looked poorer, the goats thinner, there was less wood and more rocks, yet the air was like a kiss. In such air women didn't have to be like we were on our side of the mountain. Where we have wild raspberries in ruined pine forests, I told myself, they have grapes on vines which grow between apple trees! For the first time in my life I was envious.

Did you notice the Saumua coming down to Aosta? he asked.

No.

It's the biggest truck since the war. Takes a load of thirty tons.

We arrived back before it was dark. I was in time to shut up the chickens and take the milk on my back to the dairy. My behind was sore, my hands were grimy, my hair was tangled. It took me hours to untangle it before I went to sleep. But I was proud of myself. I'd been to Italy.

We'll do another trip, Michel proposed.

School begins next week.

You're a funny one, Odile, there's no school on Sunday.

No, I said, thanks for this time.

You're a good passenger, I'll say that for you.

Are there bad ones?

Plenty. They don't trust the driver astride the machine. You can't ride a bike if you don't let go. I'm willing to bet you weren't frightened for a moment, Odile. You had confidence, didn't you? You weren't frightened for a moment, were you?

Maybe yes and maybe no. His sureness made me want to tease him.

A weekend, two months later, I was coming home from Cluses and the bus driver said:

Have you heard what happened to Michel?

Michel who?

49

Michel Labourier. You didn't hear about his accident?

On his motorbike?

No, in the factory.

What happened?

Lost both his legs.

Where is he?

Lyons. It's the best hospital in the country for burns. A military hospital. They used to fight wars with lead, now they fight them with flames. Both legs gone.

I stared through the bus window and I saw nothing, not even the factory when we passed it. The next day I went to see his mother.

Perhaps it would have been better, she said, if it had killed him outright.

No, I said, no, Madame Labourier.

He's not allowed visitors, she said, he's in a glass cage.

I'm sure you'll be able to visit him soon.

It's too far. Too far for anyone to go.

Is he still in danger?

For his life, no.

Don't cry, Madame Labourier, don't cry.

I cried when I thought about it every evening for a week in Cluses. For a man to lose both legs. I thought too about what the boys call their third leg. When you're young and both your legs are supple your third leg goes stiff . . . when you're old and your legs are stiff, your third leg goes limp. And this silly joke made me cry more.

New Year's Eve, 1953, I spent at home. Father's chair was empty. After supper Régis and Emile got up to go to the dance in the village. Come on, Odile, said Emile. I'll stay with Mother. You like dancing! insisted Emile. There's no boy in the village good enough for our Odile now, said Régis. They left. Mother sewed and went to bed early. I heard the bells pealing at midnight on the radio and the crowds cheering. I wasn't sleepy and so I let myself out and walked once round the orchard. The grass was as hard as iron. The bise had been blowing for several days and the sky was clear. Looking up at the stars, I thought of Father. Nobody can look up at the stars when they are so hard and bright and not think that they don't have something to say. Then I thought of Michel without his legs and the Red

51

Star he wore on his leather jacket. In their silence I missed his jokes and his cough. I went to check that the chicken house was well shut. When it was minus fifteen for a week on end, the foxes would cross the factory yard looking for food. A month earlier the night shift had killed a wild boar behind the turbine house. Suddenly the wind changed and to my amazement I heard dance music. A tune from a band wafting towards me. It seemed to come in waves, just as the stars seemed to twinkle. Distance and cold can do strange things. I made up my mind. I returned to the house, put my hair in a scarf, and found an old army coat. I would go and see what was happening at the Ram's Run.

Every New Year's Eve the Company imported a band to the factory and the men who were lodged in the Barracks had their own dance. The villagers didn't participate, the Company didn't encourage them to, and it was for this reason that it was called the Ram's Run. I crossed the railway line. The music was louder. The furnaces were throbbing as usual. The smoke from the chimney stacks was white in the starlight. Otherwise everything was still and frozen. Not a soul to be seen outside. The ground-floor rooms adjoining the office block were lit up. There were no curtains and the windows were misted over.

I crept up to one and scraped like a mouse with my fingernail. I couldn't believe my eyes, there was a man who was dancing sitting down on the floor! He had his hands on his hips and he threw out his feet in front of him and his feet came back as fast as they went out, like balls bouncing off a wall. I was so amazed I didn't notice the approach of the stranger who was now at my side looking down at me.

Good evening, he said. Why don't you come into the warm?

I shook my head.

You must be hot-blooded, not to mind the cold on a night like this!

It's only minus fifteen, I said.

Those were the first words I spoke to him. After them there was a silence. The two of us stood there by the light of the window, our breaths steamy and entwining like puffs from the nostrils of the same horse.

What's your name?

Odile.

Your name in full?

Mademoiselle Odile Blanc.

He stood to attention like a soldier and bowed his head. He must have been two metres tall. His hair was cropped short and he had enormous thumbs, his hands pressed against his thighs, his thumbs were as big as sparrows.

My name is Stepan Pirogov.

Where were you born?

Far away.

In a valley?

Somewhere which is flat, flat, flat.

No rivers?

There's a river there called the Pripiat.

Ours is called the Giffre.

Blanc? Blanc means white like milk?

Not always – not when you order vin blanc!

White like snow, no?

Not the white of an egg! I shouted.

Give me one more joke, he said and opened the door.

I was standing in the vestibule of the Ram's ballroom. After the glacial air outside, it felt very warm. There was the noise of men talking – like the sound of the fermentation of fruit in a barrel. There was a strong smell of sour wine, scent, and the red dust that in the end powders every ledge and every flat surface facing upwards in the factory. Along one wall of the vestibule – which was really an anteroom to the offices, where the clerical staff took off their coats and put on their aprons – there was a long table where women whom I'd never seen before were serving drinks to a group of men who had obviously been drinking for a longer time than was good for them. My brother said that the women for the Ram's Run were hired by the company and brought from far away, somewhere near Lyons, in a bus.

I wanted to get out into the air and I wanted him not to forget me immediately. So I told him a story about my grandmother. It wasn't strictly my grandmother. It was the woman my grandfather lived

with after his wife was dead. When he died, Céline – she was called
– Céline continued to live in Grandfather's house alone. She was old
by then. You can't explain all that to a stranger whom you've just
met a few minutes before and who has taken you into a bar full of
men with the windows steamed up and the floorboards muddy and
wet with melted ice. So I told him it was my grandmother.

Grandma always had a billygoat, so the neighbours had the habit
of bringing their goats to her when they were in heat. She used to
charge a thousand a visit, and if the goat didn't take they had another visit for nothing. One year, every single neighbour who had come
with a goat in heat demanded a second visit. Something was wrong.
Grandmother talked about it to Nestor the gravedigger who was
married to her niece and bred rabbits whose skins were sold as otter.
It's simple, he said to her, he's too cold, in your stable all alone, the
he-goat must be freezing. Build him a stall where he'll keep warm!
Grandma went home and thought about Nestor's advice and decided it was too much trouble. Instead, she'd bring the beast into the
kitchen – except when the sun was out. The he-goat recovered and
all the neighbours' goats were going to have kids at Eastertime.
When Grandma next saw Nestor the gravedigger, she thanked him
for his advice. So you built him a stall? he said. Too much trouble,
she replied, I brought him into the kitchen. Nestor looked surprised.
And the smell? he asked. Grandma shrugged her shoulders. What do
you expect with a he-goat, she said, he soon got used to it!

I was glad when he laughed. Then I caught sight of myself in a
mirror above the sink. What was I doing here? Quickly I turned
away from the mirror. He stood there, towering above me, protec-
tive like a tree. And hesitating. Perhaps under the neon light I was a
surprise to him. Perhaps outside he had thought I was older. Perhaps
he hadn't seen how ridiculous my clothes were. Despite myself I
glanced at the mirror again.

Your feet must be cold, he said.

I looked down at my thick, artificial-fur-lined boots and shook
my head.

If we dance, they'll warm up! And at that moment the band,
whom I couldn't see, started to play. A polka. This man, to whom
I'd told the story about the goat, took my arm and delicately guid-

ed me towards the Ram's Run. The band were installed on planks laid on scaffolding. All the other women wore high-heeled shoes. The music sounded strange, for the room, which was normally a storeroom, had no ceiling. Far up, high above, were the iron girders of the same roof which covered the topmost furnace. Most of the women were wearing low-cut dresses and some wore golden bracelets. There were also men dancing with each other. And one woman dancing alone with a gigantic feather.

What's so surprising about music is that it comes from the outside. It feels as if it comes from the inside. The man who had clicked his heels and announced his name as Stepan Pirogov was dancing with Odile Blanc. Yet inside the music, which was inside me, Odile and Stepan were the same thing. If he had touched me whilst we were dancing like men touch women, I'd have slapped his face. Behind the band there was a heap of shovels, if he had touched me, I would have taken a shovel to him. He knew better. He didn't interfere with what the music was doing. He tossed back his head at each beat, chin flung up, neck taut, mouth smiling. When the band stopped, he lifted his hand off my shoulder and stared at the players as if surprised that there was no more music, then he nodded and the band started up again. It looked as though he ordered the music with a nod of his head.

For a long while, I didn't know how long, before we had exchanged anything except a silly story about a goat, before anything had been decided between us, when I knew nothing of Stepan Pirogov, the two of us let the music fill us like a single cart drawn uphill by a cantering horse.

Are you thirsty? he eventually asked.

We returned to the vestibule with its neon lights, where he bought me a lemonade. This time I avoided looking in the mirror. His accent was very foreign.

Where is it you live, Odile?

In the house after the shunting line stops.

Where the cows are? My father kept a cow.

Just one?

Just one, outside Stockholm.

Were you born in Stockholm?

I don't know where I was born.

Your mother could tell you.

I never knew my mother.

She's dead?

No.

In the heat and the smell of sour wine and the din of the men's laughter in the Ram's Run, I suddenly felt a kind of pity for him. Or was it a pity for both of us? I gazed at the lemonade in the bottom of my glass. I could feel him looking down at me – like a tree at a rabbit. I raised my head. My sudden fear had gone.

I've been here three months, he said.

And before?

Before I was on a ship.

A sailor?

If you like.

You won't stay here long if you're a sailor!

I'd stay long for you, he said.

You know nothing about me!

I've known you since I was first conceived in the womb of a mother I never knew. He pronounced this extraordinary sentence in a strange singsong voice.

I have to go, I said.

Spend a little more of the year with me, Odile.

Is that how you talk in your language? I asked.

In my language I'd call you Dilenka.

It was different dancing with him the second time. I'm dancing with a sailor, I kept telling myself. If Mother knew I was dancing with a sailor.

I've never seen the sea in my life. When the dance was over, I went to fetch my coat.

I have to work tomorrow, I told him.

Can I see you on Saturday afternoon?

I may have to work, I don't know.

I'll be waiting for you by the footbridge, he said.

What time? I could have bitten off my tongue for saying that.

I'll be there the whole afternoon, listening to the river till you come. He said this in the same singsong voice.

My mother was washing out a bucket in the stable and I was milking before taking the bus to Cluses, it was still dark – and she screamed at me:

You would never have dared do that, if your father was still alive!

Do what?

Go to the Ram's Run!

There was no harm in it, Mother.

And to come back at four in the morning!

Three!

No one goes to the Ram's Run!

They're not beasts.

What did I do – what in God's name did I do – to deserve a daughter like you?

You did with Papa – may he rest in peace – what most wives do, Mother.

Listen to her! my mother was screaming. She talks like that to her own mother.

She hurled the bucketful of water at me. It was so cold it took my breath away and the shock of it made me fall off the stool. Lilac calmly turned her head to see what had happened. Cows are the calmest cows in the world, was one of Stepan's jokes. He would say it in a mournful voice.

I kept him waiting the whole afternoon by the footbridge. When at last I arrived, he didn't complain. He stood there listening and whilst I talked, he fingered the fringe of the scarf I had round my neck. It was so cold, the sound of the river was as shrill as the train's whistle. A train came once a fortnight to take away the molybdenum and manganese. Always at night. And since my earliest childhood the train woke me up. We walked across the lines to the big furnace shop.

Do you know each furnace has a name? he asked. The big one there is called Peter. The other one is called Tito . . . Why does it make you smile?

They weren't called those names when I was young.

Now he was smiling.

There's another called Napoleon. Why does it make you smile?

A little smile, I said.

Not so little now! he said.

Smaller than yours!

Do you know how to measure a smile?

Yes, I said.

He bent down and picked me up so my mouth was level with his, and he kissed me. On the nose.

I know so little about him, yet with the years of thinking I have learnt a great deal more from the same few facts. Perhaps there are never many facts when you first love somebody. The facts are what destiny has in store for you. His foster parents were Ukrainians and left Russia in the early twenties to settle in Sweden. One day a Russian who knew his foster mother when she was in Kiev arrived with a swaddled bundle. In it was a two-month-old baby. The couple gave the baby their family name of Pirogov. They had no children of their own. The "father" was a chairmaker and the "mother" took in washing. They had had to leave their country because in 1918 the man had joined the wrong army – the green not the red one. His "father" joined the army of a man whom Stepan called Batko Makhno. Batko, he said, meant Father. I didn't understand much.

The winter passed slowly. One Saturday we went for a walk in the snow. He was wearing blue wool mittens. As we walked, his arm round my neck and one of his huge blue woollen hands on my shoulder, he told me a story.

Once there were two bears asleep under a rock. Their fur was all white with hoarfrost. The smaller of the two opened her eyes.

Mischka! she growled.

Mouchenka! growled the other.

We can speak! Say something. Say a word.

Honey, he growled.

Snow, she said.

Spring, he said.

Death, she said.

Why death? asked Mischka.

As soon as we speak, we know death.

God! said Mischka and pushed his muzzle into her neck.

Why does God have so little power? asked Mouchenka, and placed a paw on his back.

send Odile to Cluses.

You said she's causing no trouble, Mademoiselle. At least that's what I understood, what sort of trouble?

Mademoiselle Vincent took off her hat and laid it on her lap. Her greying hair, a little damp, was pressed against her scalp.

No trouble, she said slowly, I want her to go to Cluses for her sake.

How for her sake?

If she stays here, Mademoiselle Vincent went on, she'll leave school next year. If she goes to Cluses she can continue until she gets her CAP. Let her go to Cluses. She was fanning herself with a little notebook taken from her handbag.

She'd have to be a boarder? asked Father.

Yes.

Have you mentioned it to her?

Not before talking to you, Monsieur Blanc.

He shrugged his shoulders, looked at the barometer, said nothing.

Mademoiselle Vincent got to her feet, holding her hat.

I knew you'd see reason, she said, offering him her hand like a present.

I was watching through the stable door.

Nothing to do with reason! shouted Father. In God's name! Nothing to do with reason. He paused, gave a little laugh, and leered at Mademoiselle Vincent. She was an old man's last sin – I wonder if you can understand that, Mademoiselle – his last sin.

It will mean a lot of work, she said.

Don't push her too hard, said Father, it won't change anything. You'll see I was right one day. Odile will be married before she's eighteen. At seventeen she'll be married.

We can't know, Monsieur Blanc. I hope she goes

He said it smiling, but I couldn't bear him saying it. I couldn't bear the silence of what it meant. I said the first thing that came into my head: I won't marry a man unless I love him, and if I love him, he'll love me, and if we love each other . . . if we love each other, we'll have children, and I'll be too busy to notice if he drinks, Papa, and if he drinks too much too often I'll fetch him cider from the cellar, so many glasses he'll go to sleep in the kitchen and I'll put him to bed as soon as the cows are fed.

The Barracks below are scarcely visible in the snow. I can spot them because of blue smoke coming from a chimney. A woman is crossing the footbridge over the river. The Barracks were three minutes' walk from the factory – the same as our house in the opposite direction. From our house to the footbridge was five minutes' walk. Three if I ran. Mother often sent me to the shop by the Barracks to buy mustard or salt or something she'd forgotten. I walked to the bridge and then ran. At whatever time of day, the men who lived there would cry out and wave. They worked on shifts, and of those not working or sleeping some would be washing their clothes on the grass, some preparing a meal by an open window, some tinkering with an old car they hoped to put on the road. In the winter they lit bonfires outside and they brewed tea and roasted chestnuts. They were forbidden to fish in the river.

If I stopped running they held up their arms and grinned and tried to pat my head. I was always relieved to cross the bridge back to our side. Father said the Company had built the Barracks to house a hundred men as soon as the factory was finished. The Company knew they wouldn't find more than two or three hundred local workers and so they foresaw from the beginning that they would need foreigners. Every man who lodged in the Barracks had his own secrets. Three, four, perhaps more. Impenetrable and unnameable. They turned over these secrets in their hands, wrapped them in paper, threw them in the river, burnt them, whittled them away with their knives when they had nothing else to do. Hundreds of secrets. We in the village on our side of the river had only four. Who killed Lucie Cabrol for her money? Where above Peniel is the entrance to the disused gold mine? What happens at the bridegroom's funeral before they put him in his coffin? Who betrayed the Marmot, who

29

was Michel's uncle, after the factory-gate meeting? Only four secrets. Across the river they in their sheds kept hundreds.

From here, river, house, sheds, factory, bridge, all look like toys. So it was in childhood, Odile Blanc.

One blazing July day in 1950, Mademoiselle Vincent, the schoolmistress, came to the house. I hid in the stable. She wore a hat whose brim was as wide as her shoulders; it was silver-grey in colour and around it was tied a pink satin ribbon.

Merde! said Father. It's the schoolteacher. Look, Louise!

I'll be slipping out, Achille, said Mother.

I have come to talk to you about your daughter, Monsieur Blanc.

Not doing well at school? Do sit down, Mademoiselle Vincent.

On the contrary, I've come to tell you she – she scratched her hot freckled shoulder – on the contrary, I've come to tell you how well your Odile is doing.

Kind of you to come all this way to tell us that. A little coffee?

Father poured coffee into a cup, took off his cap and adjusted it further back on his head.

She's never been difficult, has our Odile, he said.

Her intelligence –

I don't know how you see it, Mademoiselle Vincent, but to my way of seeing, intelligence is not –

She is a pupil of great promise.

Wait a year or two, she's only thirteen, said Father. In a year or two her promise – do you take sugar?

It's just because she's thirteen that we have to decide things now, Monsieur Blanc.

Even in my day, Father said, nobody married before sixteen!

I want to propose to you, Monsieur Blanc, that we

buckets, he boasted.

It took Papa three days to turn the earth of the garden and to dig in the manure. I helped him by forking the manure out of the wheelbarrow. The lilac trees were in flower and a cuckoo was singing in the forest above the factory. It was as hot as in June. Father had his shirt-sleeves rolled up, and when he was too hot, he removed his cap and he wiped his bald head, but he refused to take off his black corduroy waistcoat. Every spring he said the same thing: Do the opposite of the walnut tree! I knew the answer to his riddle: the walnut is the first to shed its leaves and the last to come out in leaf.

The garden was almost dug. Its brown earth was raked and drying in the sun. The first green shoots would soon be appearing in straight rows without a fault, because, just as at school we drew lines in pencil in our exercise books to write our words on, so Mother made a line on the earth with a string when she planted her rows of seed.

My fork had three metal prongs like any other pitchfork, but its wooden shaft was shorter so it was easier for me to handle. Father had made it for me. All the year it leant against the wall by the tap in the stable, ready for when I helped him clean out the stable after the evening milking, my homework done.

Often he complained about my handwriting, and it's true it was not as good as his. He wrote with loops and curlicues as if the whole word were a single piece of string.

The rain does better on the window pain, Odile, write it again!

In the garden he straightened his back, looked at me slyly and said: When you marry, Odile, don't marry a man who drinks.

There isn't a man who doesn't drink! I said.

Fetch me a glass of cider from the cellar, he ordered me, from the barrel on the right.

He drank the cider slowly, looking at the mountains with snow still on them.

I'd give a lot, Odile, to see the man you're going to marry.

You'll see him all right, Papa.

He shook his head and gave me back the glass. No, Odile, I'll never see the man you marry.

27

Our house had three rooms. The kitchen where everything happened and I did my homework. The Pele where my two brothers slept. And the Third Room where my parents and I slept. In the summer, after we'd brought the hay in, my brothers sometimes liked to sleep in the barn. Then I'd move into the Pele and sleep there alone. Opposite the bed hung a mirror with a black-spotted glass. When I couldn't sleep I lay there and talked to myself. I talked to my little finger. What was in the Beginning? I asked. Silence. Before God created the world and there was no earth, no manganese, and no mountains, what was there? The finger wagged. If you see a spider on a table and you brush him off, the table's still there, if you take the table outside, there's still the floorboards, if you take up the floorboards there's still the earth, if you cart the earth away there's still a sky with stars on the other side of the world, so what was there at the beginning? The finger didn't reply and I bit it.

White the page of the world below. Like the traces of tiny animals in the snow, the scribbles of what I knew as a child. Nobody else could read them here. I can see the roof, the pear tree by the shit-house, the byre we stored wood in with hives on the balcony – the basin where I washed sheets for Mother is filled with snow, for there's no trace of it – the garden beneath the windows, the little orchard, and surrounding all, as a floor surrounds a cat's saucer, the factory grounds. Every year a man came to the school to explain to us children why the factory was built where it was and why it was the pride of the region. Men had come from New York, he said, to visit it! Then he drew on the blackboard the course of the river. His was white on black and the one below is black on white. The river goes through the factory. The factory squats on the river like a woman peeing. He didn't say that.

Around the beginning of the century, he told the schoolchildren, men everywhere in the world were dreaming of a new power which was the power of electricity! This new power was hidden in our mountains, in their white waterfalls. They called the waterfalls White Coal! He made it look simple on the blackboard. Engineers canalised the water in cast-iron pipes which were two metres in diameter. They let the water, once captured, fall vertically until it acquired a pressure of 100 kilos per square centimetre, and with this pressure the water of our waterfalls turned giant wheels in turbines, which, turning, produced nine million kilowatts of electricity per hour. The beginning of electro-metallurgy in Europe! he cried. *Vive la République!*

Its work done, the river rejoined its course and made its way to the sea. Do the fish go through the turbines? a child asked. No, no, dear, answered the man. Why not? We have filters.

He doesn't know what a stupid old man he looks, Papa, leading his four miserable cows through a factory yard four times a day!

We're over the factory. When we veer to the north I can smell the fumes in its smoke.

One night I went out to lock up the chickens and I found Father by the pear tree staring up at the sky and the flames flicking out of the top of the tallest chimney stack, almost half as tall as the cliff face behind it.

Look, Odile, he whispered, look! It's like a black viper standing on its tail – can you see its tongue?

I can see the flames, Papa, some nights they're blue.

Venom! he said. Venom!

Whenever I went near the factory, I saw the dust. It was the colour of cow's liver, except that, instead of being wet and shiny, it was a dry kind of sand: it was like dried liver, pulverised into dust. The big shop was taller than any pine tree and when one of the furnaces was opened, the hot air as it rose would make a draught so that high up, by the topmost girders, a breeze would blow the dust off all the ledges and you'd see a trailing cloud like a red veil hiding the roofing. This dust astonished and fascinated me. It turned the hair of all the men who didn't wear hats slightly auburn.

The men who worked in the factory smelt of sweat, some of them of wine or garlic, and all of them of something dusty and metallic. Like the smell of the lead in a pencil when it's sharpened. For my work at school I had a pencil sharpener in the form of a globe, it was so small you couldn't tell the countries, only the difference between land and sea.

11

There was a riddle I liked as a child: four point to the sky, four walk in the dew and four have food in them; all twelve make one – what is it?

A cow, answered Régis, my elder brother, sighing loudly to show he had already heard the riddle many times before.

Odile, how is it a cow? asked poor Emile, my younger brother. People would take advantage of Emile all his life. His laziness was not so much a sin as a sickness. Each time I was pleased that Emile couldn't remember the riddle; it offered me the chance of explaining.

A cow has two horns, two ears pointing up, four legs for walking on, and four teats!

Six teats! cried Régis.

Four with milk in them!

Mother encouraged Régis to work with the furnaces because she was worried about Emile; it was going to be difficult for Emile to find a job anywhere, and so it made more sense if Emile was the one to stay at home with Father.

Father was against any son of his working in the factory. Régis would do better to go to Paris like men had done as long as anyone could remember. Long before the Eiffel Tower, long before the Arc de Triomphe, long before factories, they had gone to Paris to stoke fires and to sweep chimneys, and in the spring they had come back, money in their wallets, proud of themselves! Nobody could be proud of working – there. Father pointed with his thumb out of the window.

Times change, Achille, you forget that.

Forget! First, they try to take our land, then they want our children. What for? To produce their manganese. What use is manganese to us?

When Father was out in the fields, Régis said:

Three thousand metres above the earth – he said he could climb to five thousand, I don't know whether he was boasting – with nothing but air between us and what we can see below and I'm not frightened! The moment our feet left the ground, the wind was there. The wind is holding us up and I feel safe, I feel – I feel like a word in the breath of a voice.

She left us alone in the garden. I started hunting for snails and I forgot Claire as I followed the track down to the river behind the furnaces. When my mother came back she found my baby cousin alone in the cradle under the plum trees.

The eagle could have come! she screamed, and pecked her poor eyes out!

She ordered me to pick some nettles, and stood over me whilst I did so. I remember I tried to protect my fingers by pulling down the sleeves of my pullover to cover my hands. The bunch of nettles I'd picked lay on the bench beside the water tap outside the door, waiting for my father to return.

You have to punish Odile, my mother said to him when he arrived and she handed him a cloth to hold the nettles with. She pulled up my pinafore. I was wearing nothing underneath.

Father stood there, still as a post. Then, picking up the nettles, he held them under the tap and turned on the water.

Like this it'll hurt less, he said. Leave her to me.

My mother went indoors and my father flicked the water from the nettles onto my backside. Not a single nettle touched me. He saw to that.

Christian

I thought I would be frightened and I am not. Since he was a small boy he was a son I could trust. Christian never did crazy things like the others and he was always reassuring. He inherited a lot from his father. I'll never forget, for as long as I live, the time when he grew his first moustache. I couldn't help crying out, he looked so much like his father. Perhaps the craziest thing Christian has ever done, at least amongst the things I know about, is to bring me up here. You're sure you're ready, Mother? Yes, my boy, I answered. And he screwed up his face as if he were in pain. Perhaps he was laughing.

The first sounds I remember are the factory siren and the noise of the river. The siren was very rare and probably that's why I remember it: they only sounded it in case of an accident. It was always followed by shouts and the sound of men running. The noise of the river I remember because it was present all the while. It was louder in the spring, it was quieter in August, but it never stopped. During the summer with the windows open you could hear it in the house; in the winter, after Father had put up the double windows, you couldn't hear it indoors, but you heard it as soon as you went outside to have a shit or to fetch some wood for the stove. When I went to school I walked beside the sound of the river.

At school we learnt to draw a map of the valley with the river coloured in blue. It was never blue. Sometimes the Giffre was the colour of bran, sometimes it was grey like a mole, sometimes it was milky, and occasionally but very rarely, as rare as the siren for accidents, it was transparent, and you could see every stone on its bed.

Here there's only the sound of the wind in the sheet flapping above us.

Once my mother told me to look after my baby cousin, Claire.

4

Before the poppy flowers, its green calyx is hard like the outer shell of an almond. One day this shell is split open. Two green shards fall to the earth. It is not an axe that splits it open, simply a screwed-up ball of membrane-thin folded petals like rags. As the rags unfold, their colour changes from neonate pink to the most brazen scarlet to be found in the fields. It is as if the force that split the calyx were the need of this red to become visible and to be seen.

Seen from the height I'm now at, Father's refusal to sell his farm to the factory looks absurd. We were surrounded. Every year Father was obliged to lead his four cows through an ever larger factory yard over more railway lines. Every year the slag mountains were growing higher, hiding the house and its little plot more effectively from the road and from its own pastures on the other side of the river. The owners first doubled, then trebled, the price they were prepared to pay him. His reply remained the same. My patrimony is not for sale. Later they tried to force him out by law. He said he would dynamite their offices. Now the snow covers all.

My job was to feed the rabbits. In the early spring it was dandelions. Father said there was no other valley in the world with as many dandelions as ours. Dandelion millionaires, he called us. Rabbits eat with such impatience, as if they are eating their way towards life! Their jaws munching the dandelion leaves was the fastest thing I'd ever seen and their muzzles quivered as fast as their jaws munched.

There was a black buck rabbit I hated. He had something evil in his eye. He was always waiting for his evil moment to come and he nipped me with his teeth more than once. Mother stunned the rabbits and strung them up by their hind legs and gouged out their eyes with a knife and they bled to death. When she did this it was always on a Friday, because a rabbit, roasted in the oven with mustard, was a feast to be eaten on Sunday, when the men could stay at the table drinking gnôle after lunch and not go to work.

You can drink two litres of cider and never piss a drop – it all comes out in sweat, Achille my boy, on the furnaces.

I tried to persuade Mother to kill the black rabbit. He's our only big buck, she said. Eventually she cooked him. And to my surprise, I couldn't eat anything. She must be coming down with something, Father said. I couldn't eat because I couldn't stop thinking of how much I hated him.

The moment the snow disappeared, Mother started to nag Father. They're digging their gardens up at Pessy, she'd cry. It's too soon to plant, he'd say, without looking up from his newspaper, the earth's not warm enough. We're always the last! she complained. And our cauliflowers last year? My cauliflowers were as big as

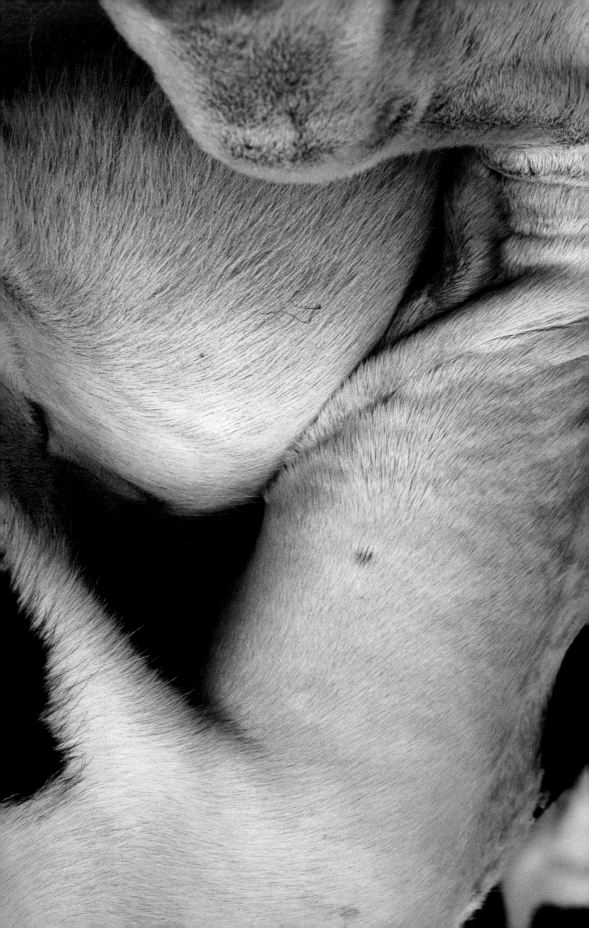

How should I know?

Everything that exists hides him, she said.

He's in his lair, he said.

He could come out, couldn't he? complained Mouchenka. Mouchenka moved her head from the shelter of the rock and the snow fell on her large black muzzle. Mischka, why does he have so little power?

Because he created the world, growled the bear.

So he spent all his power doing that and has been exhausted ever since! She blew the snow off her mouth.

No, said Mischka.

What do you mean, No?

He could have created everything differently so it did exactly what he wanted.

That would have been better?

Yes.

For a long while the two bears said nothing. At last the she-bear said: If it did exactly what he wanted, no one would recognise him! Don't you see? There'd be no need to recognise him. There'd be nothing else but him!

Mouchenka! You were simpler when you couldn't speak.

As things are, she went on, he hopes to be recognised all the while. Keeps sending reminders. Look at the snow falling, Mischka, it's falling on every pine needle.

He's clever, growled the he-bear, he's made it all so he stays hidden! He scratched the fur on her hip with his paw. He's made it all so he can be left in peace!

No, no, said Mouchenka, God made the world as it is, so he should be needed. It's what he wanted.

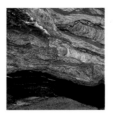

At that very moment two shots rang out, and a hunter shouted: Bagged the two of them!

The blood of the two bears stained first their fur and later the snow.

Christian

Christian is pointing at something below. He is wearing the woollen gloves which I knitted for him. I can't make out what he's pointing at.

The next weekend I suggested Stepan should come to the house. I told him about my brothers. I was hoping that if Mother saw him she might relent a little. Since the morning when she had thrown the water in the stable, she hadn't addressed a single word to me.

Not yet, Dilenka, not yet. You take a man home for the first time and everyone looks at him and starts wondering about the future, they try him on – like a pair of trousers – to see how he fits. If I were your age, but I'm a fully grown man, a foreigner, I don't have anything here, and they'll need a lot of reassuring – it's too soon, I don't know yet where to take you. Let's wait a little.

One Saturday Stepan came to Cluses by the midday bus. He wanted to see the room in the widow Besson's house, where I lodged. This time it was I who was against the visit. The

room was too small and the bed took up half the space. Instead, I had a present for him. I'd wrapped it up in a scarf of mine, a white chiffon scarf.

What can it be? he asked.

It was a hip flask for gnôle with leather round it. I saved up for a month to buy it. Stepan had complained about the cold when he was working on the night shift.

Charge Peter with shovels, six tons, *schest*! Stay near and his heat dries up the sweat so it burns you. Step back and you freeze in the night air. Minus twenty-eight. *Minus dvadtzat vossiem.*

He taught me to count in Russian, and I learnt like boys learn to imitate birds.

Stepan

61

May a mouthful of gnôle on your night shift keep you company
between the hot and the cold! I wrote that sentence on an envelope
and I stuck the envelope to the flask before I gave it to him.

When he read the message on the envelope, he threw the flask up
in the air and caught it in one hand. We were standing in front of
the bus station in Cluses. Then he kissed me. On the mouth. Each
time it was for longer.

Father's friend, César the water-diviner, used to hold a pendulum
over a local map and wherever there was buried water in the earth,
it began to turn in circles like a duckling. Am I circling over the
Mole because on a Sunday in May Stepan and I climbed there to
pick globeflowers? A woman I could shout to on the path below is
wearing a dress I never had. How much we will be forgotten!

Whilst we climbed, Stepan told me about his childhood. I was
brought up, he said, to the smell of fish glue – the smell of the ocean
bed. And I don't know if you'll believe me but it's true: I could hold
nails between my teeth as soon as I was eating solid food. I made
my first chair when I was fifteen, and Father maintained – like a true
disciple of Makhno – he maintained it was better than any throne in
the world!

The sun was hot and it was the time of May when the grass goes
mad with growth. As a child I believed I could see it growing. The
tin roofs of the chalets when we reached the alpage were crackling
in the heat. Stepan didn't know where the noise came from.
Somebody's throwing stones! he said. There was nobody. Just the
two of us.

My father and I disagreed about one thing, he went on, only one
thing and what a thing! Stepan had never seen globeflowers before.
I picked some for him. They're like brass buttons, he said, who
cleans them? I laughed. We disagreed about one thing, he went on.
I thought of Russia as my country and I wanted to go back and my
father, who was really my stepfather, was against it. When I was
eighteen, after the victory over the Germans, I filled in the forms for
repatriation. Repatriation! he screamed at me in Russian. You
weren't even born there! You don't know anything! You have to be
Russian to be so stupid!

Stepan held five golden flowers to my shoulder and said in his

singsong voice: Five Stars! The rest is ashes. You're a General. Generalissimo Odile Achilovich!

Did you get your passport? I asked him.

No, they refused me. No homeland.

I put our bunch of flowers in a little spring so they could drink, and we lay on our backs looking up at the sky, just as now I'm on my stomach looking down on the earth. Stepan put his hand on me and started to caress me. Today I won't stop him, I said to myself. He was talking about cities, asking me which one I'd like to go to – to London, to Milan, to Rotterdam, to Oslo, to Glasgow? It had never occurred to me before that somebody could choose where to live. It seemed unnatural. No, said Stepan, it's simple with these – he held up both huge hands over my face – I can work anywhere in the world. Where, where will we go, Odile? Instead of answering him, I scrambled to my feet and ran like a wild thing down the hill towards the pine trees. When he came after me I shouted at him: You're a Bohemian! A Bohemian, that's what you are. I never want to see you again! I left him at the bus station. I wouldn't let him walk me to the widow Besson's house. I gave her the flowers and the old lady thanked me and touched my forehead. Haven't you a little fever? You look all flushed. I shook my head to hide my tears from her. Go to bed, Odile, and I'll make you some verveine tea, she said. Perhaps you had too much sun.

After the day of the globeflowers, Stepan posted me a letter. It was the only piece of writing I ever saw by him. I will look to see whether it's still in the tilleul tin. He had written everything in capitals, as children do when they are first learning. The letter said: We need go nowhere, we'll stay here, I'm arranging it, will be waiting for you by the bridge, Saturday. Mischka. I never heard him before or afterwards refer to himself as Mischka.

I was able to get home on that Friday night. Mother was still not talking to me. Emile grinned as he always grinned, and after the soup conspiratorially offered me one of his cigarettes. I was still smoking it when Régis came in. It was several weeks since I'd seen Régis. He was furious. It's got to stop, Odile, do you hear me? He was shouting very loud. It can't go on, do you hear me? You've got to put an end to it, do you hear me? If Father was alive, he'd have

63

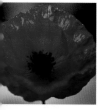

stopped you long ago, and you would have obeyed
him, do you hear me? Father wouldn't have shouted like you do, I said, and he wouldn't have
thought like you and Mother do. Don't be stupid,
Sister. Jesus, don't be stupid! Father knew I'd be
married by the age of seventeen. There was a
silence. Emile was cleaning his nails with a pock-
etknife. Do you realise that your dolt from Sweden
is married? It's a lie, you've made it up! What do
you expect, Odile, he's nearly thirty. You don't
know anything about him! We've often worked on
the same shift, we call him the Snow Shovel, he's
crap. Why do you say he's married? Listen, Sister,
to what I have to say, married or unmarried, if you
persist in going out with that shit we plan to give
him a lesson. Back to your field, Swede. He's
Russian! All the better, back behind his Iron
Curtain!

Was he a married man? The priest later asked me
when I confessed, and I had to confess further that
I didn't know, and that I'd never asked him. I went
to meet him by the footbridge the day after the
evening of Régis's threats. I told him nothing
because as soon as Stepan was there, palpable,
before my eyes, I realised that, should it come to a
fight, Régis didn't stand a chance.

We crossed the river, left the Barracks behind us,
and climbed to the forest. There we walked along
its edge until the factory and the house were out of
sight. By the old chapel with its broken windows
and the wall behind its altar pocked with bullet
marks, we turned in and crossed the forest to come
out on the path that leads to Le Mont. There we
owned a small barn for storing hay. Now it is in
ruins. I'd been there as a child with my father in the
days when he brought down hay on a sledge. In my
pocket I had the key.

I'd never before seen a man naked like Stepan. I'd seen my father and my brothers at the sink washing all over, I'd seen everything, but I'd never seen a man naked like that. The sight of him brought back to me the night I'd first met him in the Ram's Run, for I was filled with the same kind of pity – was it a pity for both of us? – and this pity was mixed with fear. Yet it wasn't with fear that my heart was pounding. My heart was pounding with excitement at the news it received: its life would never be the same again, the body it pumped for would never be the same again.

Stepan

Father was an expert grafter of fruit trees. He scarcely ever failed. Onto our wild apple trees he grafted pippins and russets, onto the wild pears, dolbos and williams. He knew at exactly which moment to graft, where to cut, how to bandage. It was as if the sap were in his thumbs. He's grafting me! I said to myself with my arms round Stepan's body. Along the new branches fruit will come like we've never known, neither he nor me. It wasn't easy for Stepan. I wasn't easy to break through. For a moment he was discouraged. I could feel it. Everything about men is so obvious that even I, at seventeen, could understand. And I shared his impatience, that's what I shared with him. So I helped him, like I used to help Father when he was grafting. I'd hold the shoot at the angle needed – whilst Father bound with the cord.

65

The sunlight streamed through the knotholes of the wall planks and the hay smelt like burnt milk and I felt that everything good that could ever happen was being grafted into me. And next week, we were eating the fruit, weren't we? If only you could have taken more! He gave us very little, dear God. Yet perhaps not. Sometimes when I tell myself the story of the two bears I say: perhaps the one thing he doesn't understand is time! How long did we lie behind the grey wood with the sunbeams? You never seemed so small as then, Stepanuschka. I was going to be your wife and the mother of your children, and the ocean which I'll never see of your ferry boat. The days were nearly at their longest. When we left, it was dark and there was a moon, we could see the path. On the way down I undid your belt. What I saw, dear God, is where? Where?

They started to build. I don't know with what words Stepan persuaded or inspired them. They started to build a room. Each shed of the Barracks was designated with a letter. I think that when they were first built the letters of the sheds went regularly from A to H. Then some man lodging there had an idea to make a joke which consisted of changing the letters. From the time I could first read as a child the eight sheds were marked IN EUROPA. I could see where the original letters had been painted over. As for the joke, the man who thought it funny had long since left and nobody now could ask him to explain. The letters remained as he had painted them. The N of the IN was written the wrong way round, И. The Company scarcely ever intruded into the Barracks area. There was only one law in the factory that counted: that the ten furnaces be tapped the required number of times every twenty-four hours, and that

the castings conform to standard when chemically analysed.

Stepan lived in shed A, which was the last one, on the edge of the factory grounds. Beyond was a plantation of pine trees. The men in shed A were building a room for Stepan. It took them a week of their free time. A partition of planks, a hole in the roof for a chimney and a new door. This room was to be separate from the rest of the dormitory, it was to be private. Stepan was making a bed, a large bed with a headboard made of oak and a carved rose at each corner. It was the first bed he'd made and it took much more time than the room. You want us to be married? he asked me. I would like to be your wife. I will marry you, he said, it's a promise.

71

Shed A is still there, the furthest from the bridge. People said he took advantage of me. They knew nothing, those people. They didn't see him carving the roses. If he didn't marry me immediately it was because he couldn't – perhaps because his papers weren't in order. Because he was already married, people said. Perhaps, long before, he did have another wife in another country, in another century. All I know is that he didn't deceive me.

One day you and I, when our grandchildren are off our hands, one day, he said, you and I will go and visit the Ukraine.

From the window of the little makeshift room at the end of shed A, I watched the swallows flying between the Barracks and the lines of spruce. It was ridiculous now for a woman living my life to still be at school, and so I left without taking any exams. As I walked away from the school for the last time through the tall wrought-iron gates, made for horsemen carrying flags, I felt Father very close. It was as if he came with me to ask for a job at the Components Factory, it was as if because of his presence they gave me a job straightaway.

My first was pressing holes in a tiny plate to fit in the back of radios. One thousand seven hundred plates a day. I wasn't badly paid and the place had the advantage of being on the riverbank. When I was ahead of my quota I could go out, smoke a cigarette, and watch the river – we were seven in the factory, seven with the boss and his son. Listening to the water, I decided how I was going to show Stepan where he could catch trout without being interfered with.

The only bad thing was the oil, it splattered my hands and wrists, I couldn't wear gloves for they slowed me down too much, and my skin was allergic to the oil. Little spots came up which itched. Stepan said that if the spots didn't go away within a week, by July 17th – I remember the date of each day of that month of summer skies, endless days, swallows, and the unimaginable – he would categorically forbid me to work there!

I kept my room at the widow's house and I spent every night IN EUROPA. On two Sundays when Stepan was working the day shift, I watched the swallows: on two Sundays when he wasn't working we stayed in bed till nightfall. He talked a lot now. In his sleep he talked in Russian. We'll stick it out another year, he said, then we'll leave and I'll find a job. You ought to make beds like this one! I told him. We'll find a house by the sea, he said. Why not by a lake? I suggested.

Sometimes he talked of the factory. I asked him if he'd heard about Michel's accident. I'd just arrived, he said, it was my first week and I was in his team. It was Peter we were tapping, and the

73

wall broke. When that happens it's like hell let loose. Hell itself, my little one. To pierce the wall you have a probe – do you know how long the tip lasts? Less than eight minutes. *Vossiem*. He was still conscious. May God help him. We got him clear and put the fireproof gown on him. He's still in hospital, I commented. With two legs gone, said Stepan.

Towards evening he shaved. I liked watching him shave. We had a jug and basin on the table by the door and he went to fetch some hot water from the bathhouse, a stone building next to the shop. Naturally I never set foot inside there. Stepan would fetch water for me to wash, and for the calls of nature I went into the plantation. This time the water was for his shaving. How much I liked to watch him shave! Perhaps any man shaving? If I'd gone into the bathhouse I'd know. It's the only moment men show their coquetry. The way they pull their skin and focus with their eyes, the noise of the blade against the stubble, the white soap on the rosy skin. After shaving, Stepan's face was softer than mine, soft as a baby's.

He was killed on July 31st.

He didn't take the leather-covered flask with
him. He left it on the table beside his shaving
brush. He was killed at four-thirty in the morning. Régis telephoned the news to the widow
Besson's house just before I was leaving for
work. I spoke to him myself. Is it certain he's
dead? Certain? Certain? I asked six times. I
went to work. The pieces I was pressing, tiny
as earrings, were for electric irons. After work
I went to the Barracks and into our room.
There was a knock on the door. I opened it.
Giuliano stood there. It was he who obtained
the oak for our bed.

Where is he? I asked, I want to see him.
Niente, Giuliano said. I want to see him, I said
again very quietly. *Niente*! he shouted at the
top of his voice. Over his shoulder I could see
other men from shed A and sheds P, O, R, U,
E, N standing at a discreet distance, looking
towards me, caps in hand, shoulders hunched.
Where is he? Giuliano's eyes filled with tears as
he shook his head. Not for a moment did he
take his eyes off me. And suddenly I understood. He had disappeared. There was no
body. Like it happens in an avalanche.

Stepan

I did not cry, Holy Mary Mother of God, I did not cry. I said to Giuliano: Who's got a motorbike in our shed? None of us. Who then? Jan in U has a motorbike. Ask him if he can take me to work tomorrow morning, I'm going to stay here.

I slept in our room. Every morning Jan took me to the Components Factory in Cluses. On the second day Emile came to the Barracks. We want you to come home, he said, and shyly, without a word, he deposited a goat's cheese on the table. Later, I told him, tell Maman and Régis I'll come home later, for the moment I must stay here.

I lay on the bed with the carved roses at each corner and stared at the planks of the roof. I found a suitcase under the bed and into it I packed his clothes, with no idea of what I was going to do with them. Perhaps his father or his wife would want them? I still did not cry. The nothingness into which he had disappeared filled me.

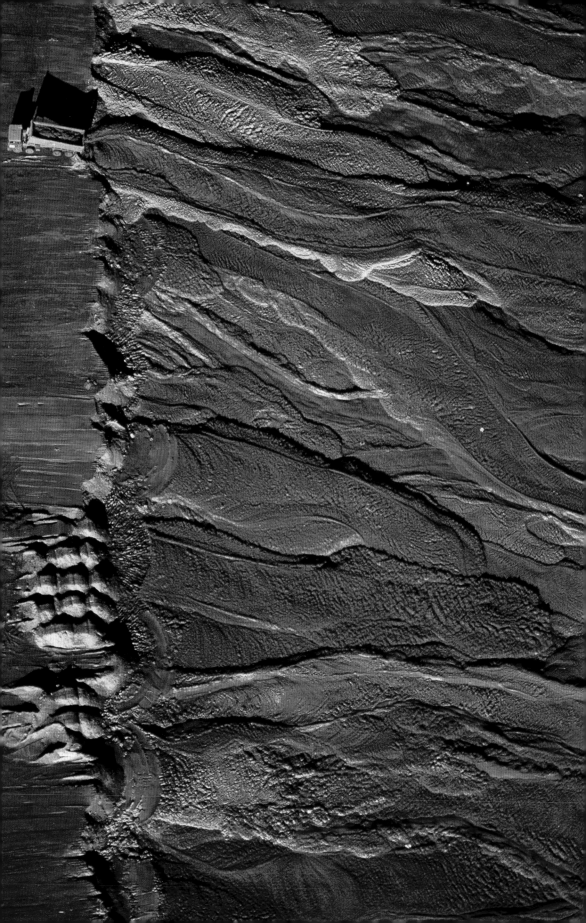

Every hour was the same.
Every minute was the same.
To piss I went into the
plantation just as I did when
his boots weren't open mouths
screaming. Odile did not
scream, she waited.
IN EUROPA, shed A.
I went on waiting.
Every evening some of
his comrades came to see me.
They came in pairs. They
brought me plates of food
which I couldn't eat. One
brought me a newspaper in a
language I couldn't understand.
They said I should go home.
They said they would come
and see me if I went home.
One of them gave me a lace
shawl in black. I folded it up.
Each day which passed
brought me more hope.
Each night I slept in the shed.
In the nothingness into which
he had disappeared, in the
nothingness in which he had
left me, I was listening for him.
And at last I heard. Now I
could go home, now I could
weep, now I could wear my
black shawl.

I went to the factory manager's office. His secretary asked me what my business was. I said it was private. Would you like to take a chair? I could hear the avalanche roar of the big furnaces. I knew that it never stopped, yet, as I sat there waiting, I thought it might. Impossible things happen. I believed that if the roar stopped I would hear his voice. On the walls were framed photographs of other factories. The frames were oak like the bed. I waited for an hour. He shouldn't be much longer, said the secretary. Where is he? He's on a long-distance call, she replied and continued her typing.

If I'd taken a back-of-the-arse, I could have done her job. Would you like some coffee? she asked. She knew me, everyone in the factory knew by now that I was Stepan Pirogov's concubine. It wasn't of course the word they used, but it was the legal term which I would have to use. Please, I said.

After another half-hour the manager saw me. His wife used to order fresh eggs from Mother. When Father was alive, Mother had to wait until he was in the fields before delivering her eggs. Food for the enemy! Father would have screamed.

He never looked at you when he was talking, the manager. It was as if he were trying to read the captions of the framed photographs on the wall. He had taken off his jacket and loosened his tie. It was hot everywhere with an August heat. I had put on a skirt and jacket so as to look more legal, and I was wearing the black shawl over my head. He motioned to the chair in front of him.

What can I do for you?

I've come about Monsieur Pirogov, Monsieur Norat.

I know. May I offer you, and the family, my sincere condolences.

81

I understand that if a worker is killed at work, the Company pays his wife a pension.

It is discretionary. We are not obliged to, and the pension terminates when and if the widow marries again.

Monsieur Pirogov was killed at work, I said.

The cause has not yet been ascertained.

Everyone knows he was asphyxiated by fumes. That's why he fell.

We will see, Mademoiselle Blanc, when the investigation is finished. I wish I could tell you more.

I have come to apply for a pension.

How old are you?

Seventeen.

And the date of your marriage, Mademoiselle Blanc? He was obliged to look at me at that moment.

We are not married.

Then I don't understand.

I lived as Monsieur Pirogov's concubine.

May I ask where?

I knew he knew where.

In shed A, I told him.

That's company property.

I want our bed too.

You want a company pension and a bed! If we gave pensions to all our workers' concubines, Mademoiselle Blanc, we'd be bankrupt!

Are there so many killed in your factories, Monsieur Norat?

I understand your distress but I'm afraid I can do nothing.

I'm pregnant. In the name of his child which I'm carrying, I'm asking, sir, for compensation.

Monsieur Norat was surprised. He left his chair and came to stand behind me.

83

Odile, if I may so call you, for you're young enough to be my daughter, I believe you, but the Company can't. From the Company's point of view, you're not married, you had no fixed residence of concubinage, and you have no proof at all that Stepan Pirogov is the father of your child.

You were born, Christian, on April 10th. You weighed 3.4 kilos, you had blue eyes, hair softer than the thistledown of a dandelion, hands smaller than Stepan's thumbs and legs like holy bread, with a zizi between them.

My mother hoped to keep you at home and put you on a bottle. I wanted to feed you myself. I had enough milk for twins. The boss at the Components Factory was obliging: so long as I did my quota, he wasn't fussy about clocking in and out. I didn't have to wait, like the others, till midday. When I felt my blouse wet on either side with milk, I left the machines thumping away and the metal shavings getting higher and higher on the shop floor. How you sucked! How you loved life! Then I had to get back early to sweep up the shavings and start again on tiny pieces for airplane hatches.

You were nearly a year old. You were taking

your first steps on the earth, and after the fourth you'd fall back onto your bottom. Funny to think of this in the sky.

Emile was playing with you under the table. Régis had been out the night before and had drunk too much. It's not the worst men who drink, the men who drink are the frightened ones, they don't know of what, we're all frightened, though at the age of eighteen I didn't know any of this. Régis was arguing with Emile, who was under the table playing with you, about whether Corneille the cattle dealer's Peugeot was dark blue or black. Emile was sure it was black. Régis was sure it was blue. They went on and on. Stop it! I cried out. You're worse than children! Régis swung round so fast I thought he was going to hit me. You keep out of this! he said. You've got enough of your own business to mind, Odile! Better think what you're going to do with your poor bastard of a kid! Shut your mouth! Emile seized Régis's legs and he fell to the ground. At that moment Mother walked in and the three of us pretended nothing had happened. When Mother left, Régis, his head in his hands, a smear of blood under his nose, muttered: Blue, Corneille's Peugeot is blue! I'm going for a walk, I said.

I walked along the rail track towards the Heaps. The last one was smoking. Soon they'll be as high as the factory, I thought. Soon they'll have covered our orchard, I thought. At home there are only three cows left. There's nothing more dead in the world than this dirt left over after burning at two thousand centigrade. Twenty-two months down in the dirt is the bastard's father. I had the courage to say those words to myself.

85

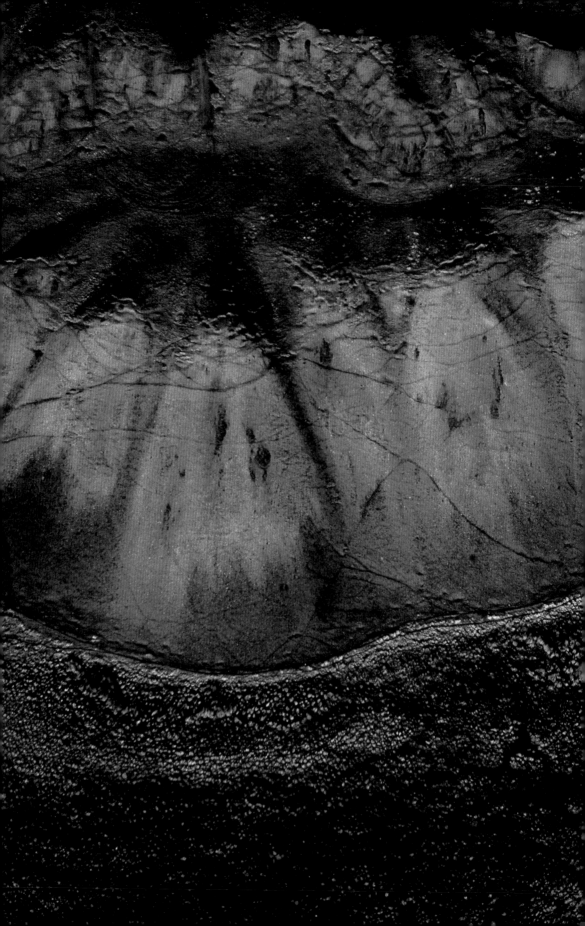

Every time I go over there to
work, Giuliano the Sardinian
told me after Stepan's death, I'm
not sure I'm going to come back.

Each wall, each opening, each
ladder was like the bone of a
sheep's skull found in the mountain – fleshless, emptied, extinct.
The furnaces throbbed, the river
flowed, the smoke, sometimes
white, sometimes grey, sometimes
yellow, thrust upwards into the
sky, men worked night and day
for generations, sweating, retch-
ing, pissing, coughing, the
Factory had not stopped once for
seven years, it produced thirty
thousand tons of ferromanganese
a year, it made money, it tested
new alloys, it made experiments,
it made profits, and it was inert,
barren, derelict. I went through
the melting shop where the furnace for manganese oxide is in
the sky, and Peter and Tito for
the ferromanganese are well
below it, yet still so high that
when the coasting cranes teem
their metal into the ladles, you
squint up at the ladles like suns
setting, and I knew how the
womb in my belly was the opposite of all I could see and touch.
Here's a woman, I whispered,
and the fruit of her womb.
I knelt on my knees. Nobody
saw me.

Horse leather is the best leather for gloves, Dilenka, it resists the heat.

I climbed up eight metal ladders, each one as high as hay in a barn, nobody stopped me, to the manganese-oxide furnace. This is where he fell. The fumes hurt my throat and I breathed deeply, yet nothing happened. I came down the eight ladders. I crossed the office space that had been the Ram's Ballroom. I found the locker where he kept his horse-leather gloves and his blue shield. It had an Italian name on it now. I laughed. I surprised myself laughing. Our love was imperishable.

Across the footbridge we lived IN EUROPA. The river was low, for the thaw had not begun. On many days it was minus ten and the mountains were still imprisoned. There was no time, I was thinking as I watched the water of the Giffre, to show Stepan where to take the trout, only time for Stepan and Odile to meet and for Christian to be conceived. Upstream, between the rocks, something attracted my attention. I waited. It seemed to me that it turned its head. A lorry clattered along the road and it flew up, long legs dangling, to perch in a pine tree. It was a heron. A water bird that nests in the top of a tree, said Stepan. I've seen three herons in my life so far. One with Father when I was small enough for him to carry me, one with Stepan on a June evening, and one that Sunday in March '56.

Stepan said the name of the heron was *tzaplia*, a creature from far away with a message. Waiting for its fish, it becomes as still as a stick. Which is why I wasn't sure when I first spotted it. From the pine tree the heron surveyed the road, the factory grounds, the tall chimneys with their heads like the open beaks of gigantic fledgelings looking up for food, the manganese-oxide furnace, Peter, Tito, the turbine house, the cliff-face and that sky where I'm flying with my son. Of its message I was ignorant.

She was in a good mood, Mother. She gave us a kilo of honey, she said your blue eyes were going to break girls' hearts, she changed your nappies. For once I wasn't in a hurry to leave and we missed the bus back to Cluses and had to hitchhike. You made hitchhiking easy. With you in my arms, the very first car stopped. The driver leant back and opened the rear door. As we were climbing in, he spoke my name. He was wearing a cap over his eyes and he had a black beard. Yet something in the way he said my name was familiar, was old. Our eyes met and suddenly I recognised him.

Michel!

He leant his head back awkwardly for me to kiss his cheek. I guessed he couldn't turn round, couldn't move his legs, so I kissed him like that.

I was so sorry, Odile, when I heard about what happened, he said. I offer you my sympathy and all my condolences.

His voice had changed. Changed more than his face on account of his beard. Before, he had spoken like most people do, his voice close-up to what he was saying. Now his voice was far away, like a priest's voice at the altar.

This is our son, Christian, I told him.

He touched your woollen bonnet with his hand and it was then I noticed the scars on it: they were violet – the same colour as molybdenum bread goes when it's cooling. Where they were violet, there was less flesh.

You're going where? he asked.

Cluses.

You live there?

I nodded. And you, Michel?

Lyons's finished with me. The surgeons say I'm a masterpiece. Do you know how many operations I had? Thirty-seven!

He laughed and slapped his thigh so the sound should remind me it was made of metal. He was wearing well-pressed trousers, light-coloured socks, polished shoes.

You started to cry.

Developing his lungs! said Michel. He can't run at his age, poor little mite, all he can do is to howl if he wants to fill his lungs. Here! Christian! Look!

He dangled a key-ring before your eyes and you leant your head against my breast and stopped crying.

And you, Michel?

I'm going to take on the tobacconist's and newspaper shop at Pouilly.

How will you manage to –

Everything, Odile, everything. I can even climb a ladder! The trade union lawyers forced them to give me a pension. I don't have to work too much.

Stupidly, helplessly and for no good reason, I began to snivel. Michel turned round and started the engine. He could drive the car, for it had been adapted and fitted out with hand-controls. His two feet in their polished shoes just rested on the floor. Like flatirons.

When there's no choice, Michel said over his shoulder, it's extraordinary what you can adapt to.

I know.

At first I was too drugged to realise, he said, then bit by bit the truth came home to me. When I woke up in the morning and remembered what I was, I wanted to scream. For a week I was in despair. Why me? I kept on asking. Why me?

I know, I said. You'd gone to sleep. We were driving along by the river. He controlled the speed with his scarred right hand. His two feet lay on the floor like flatirons. I was still sniffling.

The great thing in hospital is you aren't alone. There are other people in the same state as you, he said, some are worse off than you. You've only got one life, they say, so better make the most of it. It's not true, Odile.

I know, I said between tears.

We were all bad cases. Third-degree burns, with fifty, sixty, seventy percent disability. We'd have all been dead twenty years ago. There were people – we heard it – there were people who said we'd be better off dead. We had to learn to live a second life. The first one was over forever and ever. He's sleeping now?

He's asleep, yes, I whispered.

I had to learn how to live – and it wasn't like learning for the second time, that's what's so strange, Odile, it was like learning for the first time. Now I'm beginning my second life.

Do you have much pain? I asked.

Not much.

Never?

Not much. Sometimes when it's hot in the summer I'm uncomfortable. He touched the top of his thigh. Otherwise, no. For a long while I dreamt of pain in my legs. They weren't amputated in my dreams. I'll tell you something else, Odile. I've become a fire-cutter.

I started to laugh. As with my tears, I didn't know why.

There was an old man in the hospital. He wasn't a patient and he wasn't a member of the staff . . . he was there every day. He went out to buy whatever we asked him – papers, fruit, tobacco, eau de cologne – and in return we gave him the change. He was eighty-two. When he was younger he'd been a railwayman. He was a fire-cutter. I saw him take the pain away once. A nurse scalded her hands with boiling water, and the old man put a stop to her suffering in two minutes. According to him he was getting too old, said the effort of cutting the fire took too much out of him. So, one day he announced he'd been watching us all very carefully and now he'd decided, now he'd chosen his successor. And it was to be me. He gave me his gift.

How?

Like that.

What did he do?

He just gave me his gift.

We were in Cluses and Michel drove us to the front door. You were already asleep in my arms. Despite my protests he insisted on getting out of the car. He moved his legs with his arms. He pulled himself up with his arms. His neck and shoulders were much thicker than they had been. He extracted himself like a man climbing out of a trench he's dug. There he stood on the pavement, swaying slightly from his hips.

If you ever need me, you know where to find me now. I was so sorry, he repeated again, to hear what had happened.

Do you remember Stepan? I asked him.

I remember him. He was very tall, with blond hair. Didn't he have blue eyes? We worked a couple of nights in the same gang, two or three nights I think – before I collected this packet. He slapped his hip.

I don't even have a picture of him, I said.

You don't need a photo, he said, fingering your woolen bonnet, you have his progeny.

Strange word, progeny!

You can't have closer, he said. Good night.

The long years began, the long years of your boyhood. Do you remember the flat we lived in? You did your homework on the kitchen table. You were always wanting me to make potato pancakes for supper. You kept a soccer ball in a net hung from the ceiling over your bed. Your room smelt of glue because of the models you made. The same smell as my nail varnish. You could change washers on a tap before you were ten. In my room there was the oak bed with the carved roses, when you were ill you slept in it with me and sometimes on Sundays too. Remember when we painted the living room and you fell off the ladder? You were all I had in the world and I thought you were dead.

Why do I have the same name as you, Maman, why am I called Christian Blanc?

Because your father died before you were born.

What was he like?

Strong.

What did he look like?

Big.

Was he like me?

Yes.

Was he interested in aircraft?

Not particularly, I think.

You don't know much about him, do you?

As much as anyone ever knows.

Guess what I really want to do, Maman. I want to build a glider. One that will fly. I saw a picture in a book at school. It'll have to be big, as big as a car.

Big enough to fly us round the world?

Yes . . . I'll need lots of glue.

The long years began. Where could we go to be at home? Régis got married to Marie-Jeanne. Her condition for marrying him was that he give up drinking, and for a while he did. Mother sold the last cow, keeping only the goats and chickens. The trees of the forest, up by the path to Le Mont, began to die. The hillside above the river became the grey rusty colour of dead wood. Emile got a job loading drums in a paint factory near the frontier and Mother lavished all her attention upon him. Every evening he came home to a hero's welcome. His weaknesses inspired her determination to live to be a hundred. As she aged, Emile became the love of her life. She changed the hay of his mattress every week.

I bought an atlas to study how to go to Stockholm. I found the Ukraine and the river Pripiat. Yet what could we have done there? We'd have been further from home than ever.

Why are we going up so fast now?

The boss at the Components Factory pursued us for a while. You remember he bought you a Sputnik with a dog inside, and you lost the dog? I went to his house for supper several times. He took us to the lake and we ate a fish like a trout but stronger tasting. You said fish find their way in the ocean through their sense of smell. His wife had left him years before. He was nearly forty, you were nine.

Do you want to marry Gaston, Maman?

We are still climbing into the sky.

No, I don't want to marry him.

I think he wants to marry you.

I don't know.

He told me he's going to buy a Citroën DS.

That's what interests you, isn't it?

If you didn't have to work for him, Maman, I think I'd like him more.

Gaston is very kind. He and I don't know the same things, that's all. What he knows doesn't interest me a lot and what I know would frighten him.

You couldn't frighten me, Maman.

When we turn, Christian, it's strange, for there I am looking not up but down at the blue sky.

Michel's shop in Pouilly was unlike any other in the district. The newspapers were arranged in a special way, the left-wing ones

95

always in front. When a customer asked for *Le Figaro*, Michel bent down and brought one up from under the counter with a look of disgust, as if the paper the man had demanded were wrapped round a rotten fish. He sold bottles of gnôle with a pear the size of my fist inside the bottle.

How did the pear get inside? you asked.

It grew from a pip! Michel said and you didn't know whether to believe him or not.

He also sold toboggans and radios. He was mad about radios and could repair anything. On the back wall of the shop he pinned a large map of the world and on each country he stuck little labels like the ones they sell for jam pots, indicating the city, the wavelength, the hours of broadcasting. There were those who said that Michel with his politics and his radios could only be a spy for the Russians! His reputation as a fire-cutter spread. People from other valleys came to him to have the pain of their burns taken away. He categorically refused any payment. It's a gift! he repeated.

Do you remember when I took you to him? You'd burnt the palm of your hand with a firecracker. It wasn't serious but you were howling your head off. Michel came out from behind the counter with his stiff, swaying movement – like a skittle. Let's go into the back room, he said. I made as if to accompany you but he shook his head and the two of you disappeared. He closed the door and within seconds you stopped howling. Not gradually but suddenly in mid-cry. There wasn't a sound in the shop. Total silence. After what seemed an eternity I couldn't bear it anymore and shouted your name. You came bounding through the door laughing. Michel lumbered after you. There were already grey hairs in his black head.

You don't have to burn yourself in order to come and see me, he said when I thanked him and kissed him goodbye.

Later I asked you: What happened?

Nothing.

What did Michel do?

He showed me one of his burns.

Where?

Here – you pointed at your tummy.

And your hand stopped hurting?

No, it wasn't hurting anymore. It stopped hurting before he showed me his burn.

Why did he show it to you then?

Because I asked him.

What are we doing here, Christian, on this earth, in this sky?

I'd been working in the Components Factory for ten years. On the wall beside my bench there were thirty postcards of the Mediterranean and palm trees and cows and cherry trees in flower and a village with a steeple – all of them sent to me over the years by friends on holiday. Gaston had understood the reality of our situation. When he stood behind me, pretending to oversee my work, I could sense his regret in my shoulder blades, because I could also sense my own. The racket of the machines month after month, year after year, wore away principles. The years were long. When I didn't sleep the nights too were long.

The factory shut for the month of August. We never went away for a holiday like some of the others. I gave Mother a hand in the garden. I made jam and bottled the last of the runner beans. When I passed the factory I no longer thought of Stepan. There is nothing in the factory which can have a memory. I thought of him when I ironed your shirts and cut your hair. I thought of him too when I did my face in the mirror. I was ageing. I looked as though I'd been married for twenty years.

Do you know how to measure a smile? Stepan asked.

Yes, I said.

He bent down and picked me up so my mouth was level with his and he kissed me.

You had a friend called Sébastien, whose father was the caretaker of the holiday camp in Bakon, on the other side of the Roc d'Enfer. Some Thursdays when there was no school, you spent the day with him up there. I was glad because the mountain air did you good. Cluses is like a dungeon. When the holiday camp was full of kids from the cities in the north, you wanted to go and find out if there were any flying enthusiasts. Here, you said, people don't have a clue. Already I couldn't follow you talking about "aerofoils" and

"wing loadings". I'm not sure Sébastien understood much either. His passion was fiddling with
television sets. He could come into Michel's shop
and talk like a schoolmaster for an hour about
new transistor circuits. Sébastien was twelve and
you were eleven when in August '66 you went to
spend a whole fortnight with him up in Bakon.

I didn't have to go to work and I was by myself,
alone as I hadn't been for ten years. On the second
day I did something I hadn't done since Stepan's
death: I didn't get dressed at all, I lay in bed, I lis-
tened to the radio, I took a shower when I was too
hot, I remembered, I didn't get up. Mother would
have been deeply ashamed of me. Papa, examin-
ing the cruel crevices in his hands, would have
looked up and said with a wink: Why not, if she
can? My life already seemed inexplicably long.
The next day I spent at the swimming pool sun-
bathing. From having to stand too much at work
I was developing varicose veins. My hands
weren't like Papa's but they were red and rough. I
was never taught to swim. I made an appointment
at the hairdresser's. Mother had never once been
to a hairdresser in her life.

Coming out of the hairdresser's with a scarf
over my head, I saw Michel on the other side of
the road. He was walking on crutches. I waved
and he didn't see me. His head was down and it
looked as though the going was painful. I waited
for the traffic and then I ran across the street.
When at last he saw me, his face, red and glisten-
ing with sweat, broke into a smile.

What a surprise! Always in his faraway voice.

I've just had my hair done.

Come and have a coffee.

We went to the brasserie by the post office.

A waiter offered him a chair. Obstinately he took another.

Why don't you take off your scarf?

Order me a café au lait and I'll be back. I went to the toilet.

Ah! Odile! A beautiful head of hair you have there! All his words had to be hurled across the ravine of what had befallen him.

It's too fine. It breaks too easily.

Too fine? I wouldn't know what too fine was! He drank from his glass of white wine and lemonade. You remember the trip we made to Italy?

I nodded.

Thirteen years ago.

The only time I've ever been on a motorbike. Afterwards you told me I was a good passenger.

Your outfit has closed down for the whole month?

Like every year.

What about a trip to Paris?

Paris! It's hundreds of kilometres away.

We take the car and we take four days, there and back. I have to go anyway to get a prosthesis adjusted. It's not satisfactory . . . the left one here. If you came with me, it would be a holiday. What do you say?

It's a long way.

Don't put your scarf on again.

Are we, Christian, a mother and child flying in the sky?

Christian

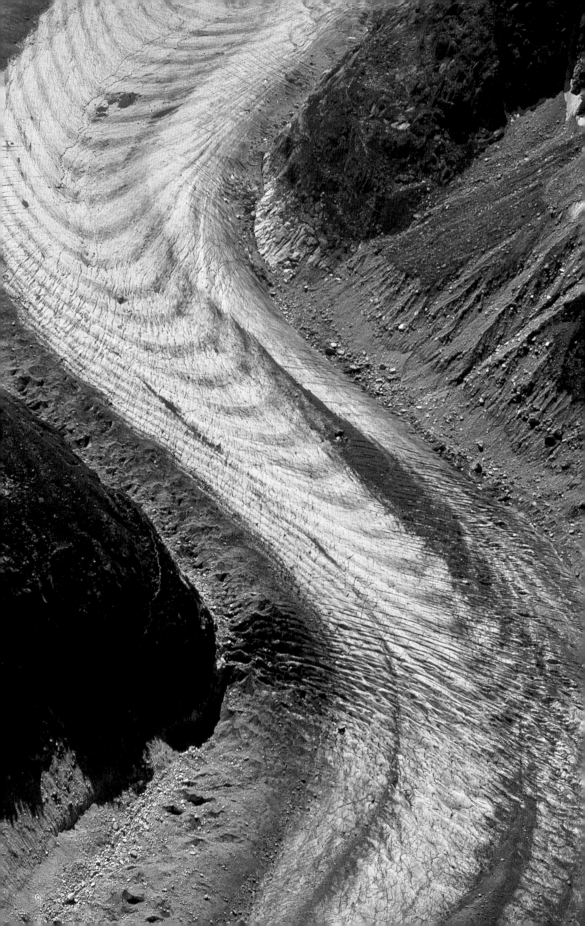

At that moment I was twenty-nine; Michel was thirty-seven. If I'd been told as a child what the life of an adult is like, I wouldn't have believed it. I'd never have believed it could be so unfinished. When young we lend so much authority and sureness to our elders. Michel and I had seen and lived a good deal, and yet, as we followed the Rhône along the gorge through the end of the Jura Mountains, we were like children. When I think of it now, I want to protect us.

It was a white Renault 4. He had covered the seats with a fabric, striped like a zebra skin. He liked putting on a strong eau de cologne which, mixed with sweat and the August heat, smelt like mule. I'd bought a pair of white net gloves for the trip. In my whole life I never dreamt of wearing gloves in the summer but I'd seen this pair in a shop in Cluses, a shop where the bosses' wives bought their haberdashery, and I said to myself: What the hell, Odile, if you're going to Paris, Paris of all places on this earth, and you've got a smart pair of white shoes, you may as well wear white net gloves in August. In addition, they were at half-price.

When I think of us on our way to Paris, I want us to come to no harm.

The white cat died last week. She was hit by a car. Michel was at the shop and I went out into the garden and I heard a meow. She was in the grass by the edge of the road. Her back was broken, so I put her to lie on a blanket by the stove in the kitchen. She lay there, her white mouth a little open and her tongue scarcely less white than her teeth. She turned – or her body turned her – onto her side with her four legs stretched out and her hind legs straight behind her, as if she were leaping. Slowly, with her two forelegs she wiped her face, moving her paws down from her ears over her eyes towards her mouth. She did this once only, rubbing the vision of life out of her eyes. When her paws reached her mouth she was dead.

Can there be any love without pity?

101

The Jura are not like our mountains. They are more morose, more resigned to their fate. They would never cover a car seat with zebra skin nor wear white gloves in August. We passed a lake which looked as though no boat had ever sailed upon it. Michel talked about General de Gaulle and I didn't know whether he hated or admired him. Next he talked about the factory. It belonged now to a multinational with factories in twenty-one different countries. TPI. The multinationals, Michel said, are the new robber barons of our time. TPI made eight thousand five hundred million francs profit in '66.

Michel keeps figures in his head like other people keep the words of songs.

It's raining kisses
and hailing caresses
till the flood of tenderness
takes the nest.

A man on one of their furnaces, he said, breathes air that contains four hundred thousand dust particles per litre – that's lethal.

May a mouthful of this on your night shift my darling keep you company between the hot and the cold ...

Lethal. No man can stand it indefinitely, Michel said. The forest is dying. The five chimneys spew out one thousand two hundred tons of fluorine waste every year.

Papa had been right about the venom. He had been right too about my being married at seventeen. What he never knew, what he could never have imagined, was that I'd be a widow by eighteen.

A TPI factory in the Pyrenees, Michel went on, has destroyed four thousand hectares of forest in three years and poisoned seven hundred and fifty cows and sheep.

What I've lost is more than seven hundred and fifty cows and sheep! I said.

You have a child. It helps.

It helps, yes, but a son doesn't make up for everything. One day he'll go.

At least you have somebody to live for.

Sometimes, I shouted, you want to live for yourself!

We each have to live for ourselves, he said.

Sometimes I look at other women and I hate them because they're, because they're . . .

Not living with a ghost?

I'm getting out, let me get out.

You have nothing to be angry about.

Nobody has the right to call him a ghost. Do you hear me, Michel? Nobody. He's here! I beat my hand on my breast.

And I'm here, Michel said banging his hands down on the steering wheel, I'm here and I have no child so I know what I'm saying when I tell you you're lucky.

Lucky? Me lucky! I'm about as lucky as you, my dear Michel.

He said nothing more. We were driving between hills of grass which rose to outcrops of rock. The sky was thundery. The cows were clustered together, heads down, wherever there was a little shade. We were both sweating and hot.

If you see a river, I said, why don't you stop? Then I remembered

103

it would be hard for him to clamber down a riverbank and I regretted saying it. Can you still have children? I asked him after five minutes' silence.

He nodded without a word.

Around the next corner was a café and we stopped. We were waiting for the sandwich we had ordered when we heard a screeching of brakes followed by a crash. I rushed to the café door. A Peugeot 304, coming too fast round the bend, had crashed into the back of our Renault. The driver, unhurt, was waving his arms and cursing everything he could see. In God's name, it's not possible!No warning for the bend! How is it possible to build such a fool road? And to park a car there you need the mind of a cunt! It's not possible, Jesus, it's not possible!

Michel walked over to his car and bent stiffly forward from the waist; he was like the conductor of a brass band after the end of a number, and he examined the damage. The other driver was pacing out the distance from the two cars to the corner and counting out loud in a shrill, mad voice. He had a way of looking at things, Michel – shafts, flanges, joints, cylinder heads, casings – which stopped them being intransigent, which made them obedient. As I watched him I thought of his gift of taking away the pain of burns. Was it a gift of attracting to himself and so dispersing a kind of shock? The shock suffered by burnt flesh or a chassis?

If we order the parts tonight, he shouted to me, it's only one day's work, we'll be on the road the day after tomorrow.

Swaying like a ninepin, he moved across to the Peugeot. The owner screamed: It's not possible! Less than twenty-eight metres from the corner, you can see my brake marks, can't you? Jesus! I jammed them on as soon as I saw you. You're a public danger. If you're a gimp you should get yourself about in a wheelchair.

I reckon, said Michel very calmly, the packet there won't cost you more than a hundred and fifty thousand – the price of a good bicycle! You're fortunate, considering the speed you were going.

Crippled cunt! the man said.

The storm hadn't broken and we had to wait for the café owner to drive us to the nearest hotel, five kilometres away.

Give us some cold beer, can you? Michel asked. The sweat lined the furrows of his brow and the pouches under his eyes. He sat on a table, his back to the wall, legs straight out, pointed polished shoes at an impossible angle, as if both ankles were broken.

On a day like this, he said to me, when you're working on the furnaces, you're working in a temperature of seventy degrees centigrade. Half-way between blood-heat and boiling point. Half-way to hell . . . He poured some beer down his throat.

I could never believe in hell, I told him. I couldn't believe any father would invent hell as a punishment for his children.

Fathers shoot their sons dead, he said.

They shoot in anger. The way I learnt, hell has to do with justice, not anger.

I offered him a handkerchief to wipe his face. He held it up before his eyes because it had flowers printed on it, and he didn't use it.

You really want to know about hell, he said smiling, it's here.

Sounds odd coming from you, Michel, the one who's always talking about change and progress . . .

I put the handkerchief carefully back in my bag.

Who says hell has to stay the same? Hell begins with hope. If we didn't have any hopes we wouldn't suffer. We'd be like those rocks against the sky.

I caught hold of the hand he was pointing with. He didn't resist and I turned it over. On the back of his fingers he has black hairs; where the violet scar is, there is no hair. I sprayed some eau de cologne onto his wrist and he withdrew his hand to smell it.

Hell begins with the idea that things can be made better, he said. It's refreshing–your scent. What's the opposite of hell? Paradise, no?

Give me your other hand.

I sprayed the back of that hand and he didn't withdraw it, it lay in my lap.

I could take you to your hotel now, announced the café owner.

The hotel backed onto a river whose bed was almost dry. The window of my room looked out onto the pebbles. It was the first time in my life I'd stayed in a hotel – which didn't prevent my realising this one was unusual. The proprietor, who was working in the kitchen when we arrived, came out wiping his hands on a sack tied round his waist.

Two rooms, yes, he said, you'll be eating here tonight? Tonight I'm cooking a dish I've never tried before!

The corridor leading to the bedrooms was stacked with wardrobes, there was scarcely space to get by. In my room, besides a bed and a washbasin there were two electric radiators and a deep freeze. I looked inside the freezer and it was full of meat. At last the rain began to fall, large drops the size of pearls. I washed and lay on the bed in my slip, with my feet bare.

I had the impression that we had lost our way: we were not going to arrive in Paris, Michel's prosthesis was not going to be adjusted, we were in a land apart, which we had come across by accident, without meaning to, and without realising it, until now we had found ourselves in a hotel run by a madman. With this idea, and yet peacefully and to the sound of the rain, I fell asleep.

Michel

When I woke up the storm had passed. I put on another dress and a pair of white shoes – the pair which had prompted me to buy the summer gloves. I also put on a necklace of coloured beads that Christian had made for me at school. It was getting dark – the short days of August for all their heat – and I could just make out the white shapes of geese down by the river. I slipped past the wardrobes and found my way downstairs.

To my surprise there were three or four other guests in the dining room. Michel was sitting at a table by the window, where there was a large vase of orange gladioli. I can still see the flowers. He had changed his shirt and washed.

So too had the proprietor, who had discarded the sack and was now wearing a tie. He led me to the table. Michel insisted upon getting to his feet. We said good evening to each other like people do in films.

Would we like an aperitif? asked the proprietor. Two Suzes, said Michel. My sense of us having lost our way reminded me of the uncertainty children feel when they find themselves having to do something for the first time. Yet I'd never felt older.

Can we propose to you, sir, poularde en soutien-gorge?

What is it? asked Michel.

A skinned chicken roasted in pastry, sir. Unforgettable. And as an entrée perhaps truite au bleu?

It's the chicken you've cooked this way for the first time? I asked.

Precisely, Madame, the first soutien-gorge I've ever fitted! He winked at Michel.

Four point to the sky, four walk in the dew, and four have food in them; all twelve make one – what is it? I asked the man.

He didn't know and I wouldn't tell him. We ate well, like at a baptism.

If you wanted, I could help you, Michel said.

What do I need help for?

To live.

I've managed not too badly up to now. It's good, this white wine, isn't it? Santé.

Do you know what people say about you?

I've never worried. It's the one thing, Michel, I've never worried about.

There's no talking with her, they say. When Odile's made up her mind to do something, she does it. When she's made up her mind not to, nothing can make her. There's no approaching her. They respect your courage, they respect the way you've brought up the boy – but from a distance. You're alone.

I don't feel it.

In a few years it'll be too late.

Too late for what?

Too late to change.

You want to change everything, Michel, the world, hell, people, politics, now me.

You think things can stay as they are?

I don't know.

Happiness doesn't say anything to you?

There's more pain than happiness, I said.

Pain, yes.

Have I told you the story of the two bears? I asked.

Who's been eating from my plate? The story of the three bears?

No, two. Two bears in the snow . . .

Fairy tales, Odile! We're too old now for fairy tales. We need to face reality.

Like we both do all the time.

Then he said something that impressed me, for he said it so slowly and emphatically: Things can't . . . go on . . . as they are. These words were more grunted than spoken and the gladioli I was gazing at in their vase blurred before my eyes.

They do go on, I replied, every day, every hour. People work, people go home to eat, feed the cat, watch TV, go to bed, make jam, mend radios, take baths, it all goes on all the while – till one day each of us dies.

And that's what you're waiting for! he said.

I'm not waiting for anything.

You know you talk like an old woman?

I'm a widow. I was a widow at eighteen.

You talk like an old woman and you're not thirty.

In three months. Very soon. You believe age makes a difference?

It's not age, it's time running out. He dabbed at his forehead with his red handkerchief.

Say it again, Michel, I taunted him, according to you things can't go on. But they do – you know it as well as I do. Things go on!

If we don't fight, he said, we lose all.

Do you really think life's only a battle?

At this he laughed, laughed till the tears came to his eyes. He filled up my glass, raised his, and we clinked them.

You of all people, Odile, not to know the answer to that question. Do you – you, Odile Blanc – really think life isn't a battle?

He laughed shortly again but this time his tears were those of sadness.

When I went up to my room, with the freezer full of meat and a reproduction of the Angelus above the bed, I didn't undress. I waited for half an hour and watched the river. Then I brushed my hair and, without putting my shoes on, I edged my way past the wardrobes in the corridor and found the door to Michel's room, which I opened without knocking.

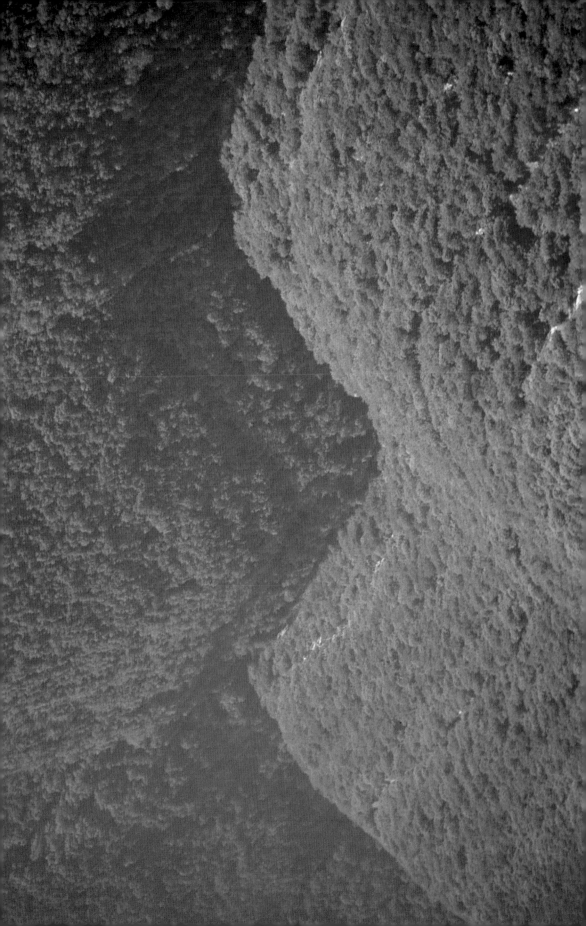

Our shadow is moving over the white snow, Christian, and looks like the twenty-seventh letter of the alphabet, something between a D and an L. In Cluses, where I learnt words off the blackboard in the school, which, after the factory, was the tallest building I'd ever seen, in Cluses words were strange to me. Now they are coming back into my head like pigeons into their pigeon loft.

From our union, Marie-Noelle was born on 4 August '67. At birth she weighed 3.2 kilos, a little less than you. The milk came up into my breasts and I fed her for more than nine months. I didn't want to stop. I was no longer working in the Components Factory, for the four of us lived together above the shop in Pouilly.

Madame Labourier knitted a pink blanket for the cradle. Odile Blanc was not exactly the daughter-in-law Madame Labourier would have chosen for her son, but facts were facts, and Marie-Noelle was her grand-daughter.

When Michel was young, Madame Labourier informed me, you couldn't count the number of girls he went out with. After the accident, during the years he was away in Lyons, they all got married. All things consid-ered, it's understandable, isn't it? After all, *they* were young healthy girls.

Later she warned me about the future. As he ages, he's going to change, he's going to become more and more demanding. I saw it with Neighbour Henri who had polio, and my poor cousin Gervais who had diabetes. As they get older, cripples – particularly men cripples – become difficult and crotchety. You'll have to be patient, my girl.

After you were born, Marie-Noelle, it was as if you gave him back his legs. He was so proud of you, his pride had feet. He hated being separated from you for more than an hour or two. When you were old enough to go to school, he refused to take the car, he walked with you a good half-kilometre, holding your hand.

The limbs he had lost were somehow returned to him in your small child's body. It was he, not me, who taught you to walk. Now you are no longer a child and from the sky I can talk to you.

Women are beautiful when young, almost all women. Don't listen to envious gossip, Marie-Noëlle. Whatever the proportions of a face, whether a body is too skinny or too heavy, at some moment a woman possesses the power of beauty which is given to us as women. Often the moment is brief. Sometimes the moment may come and we do not even know it. Yet traces of it remain. Even at my advanced age now there are traces.

Look in a mirror if you pass one this afternoon in the hearing aid shop in Annecy whilst you're waiting for Papa, look at your hair which you washed last night and see how it invites being touched. Look at your shoulder when you wash at the sink and then look down at where your breast assembles itself, look at the part between shoulder and breast which slopes like an alpage – for thirty years still this slope is going to attract tears, teeth clenched in passion, feverish children, sleeping heads, work-rough hands. This beauty which hasn't a name. Look at how gently your stomach falls at its centre into the navel, like a white begonia in full bloom. You can touch its beauty. Our hips move with an assurance that no man has; yet they promise a peace, our hips, like a cow's tongue for – her calf. This frightens men, who knock us over and call us cunts. Do you know what our legs are like, seen from the back, Marie-Noëlle, like lilies just before they open!

Marie-Noëlle

ALSO BY PATRICIA MACDONALD

Shadow of Heaven
Order & Chaos
Views of Gaia
'To remain dissolved' in Studies in Photography

WITH ANGUS MACDONALD:

Above Edinburgh
The Highlands and Islands of Scotland
Granite and Green

ALSO BY JOHN BERGER

Into Their Labours
A Painter of our Time
Permanent Red
The Foot of Clive
Corker's Freedom
A Fortunate Man
Art and Revolution
The Moment of Cubism and Other Essays
The Look of Things: Selected Essays and Articles
Ways of Seeing
Another Way of Telling
A Seventh Man
G.
About Looking
And Our Faces, My Heart, Brief as Photos
The Sense of Sight
The Success and Failure of Picasso
Keeping a Rendezvous
Pages of the Wound
Photocopies
To the Wedding
King

Look, look down there – can you see? – there's a heron flying. *Tzaplia*, the last message before nightfall.

Tell them, Christian, tell them when we land on the earth that there's nothing more to know.

Often the burnt come to the shop to have their pain taken away. Michel insists on being alone with them, I have never seen what he does. Sometimes somebody asks him to go down to an accident in the factory. Once or twice he has succeeded in taking the pain away by telephone. Four years ago, Louis's son, Gérard, was pruning an apple tree with a chain saw, standing on a ladder. Somehow he slipped and the chain saw, still turning, touched his neck before clattering to the ground. Blood was pouring out of a jugular vein into his shirt. He came running into the shop, his face like a sheep's. Michel stopped the bleeding within a minute without touching the wound. Then he sent Gérard down to the doctor, who couldn't believe his medical eyes.

Each time he takes away the pain he is exhausted afterwards, and, when I'm there, I massage the back of his neck and shoulders to give him relief. One night when I was doing this to him, he said: Paradise is rest, isn't it? Repose. You go to paradise after you've worked three shifts running, twenty-four hours without a break. You stop and there's the pure pleasure of stopping, doing nothing, lying down. Paradise is doing fuck-all. You don't know anything else exists. No relations in paradise, Odile, no children, no women, no men. Undistilled egotism, paradise! Isn't that it, my love? I went on massaging him and I felt his cart-horse shoulders relaxing, accepting. After a while he turned towards me, his eyes piercing me, and he pronounced my name. Then he took me in his arms, and he carried me, yes, he carried me to the bed and murmured: It's only in hell, my love, that we find each other!

And Michel found me there on the bed. He found Odile.

Michel

119

legless. The two stumps are the colour of molybdenum bread when it's cooling before the spray rains on it. Only their colour is like molybdenum. The specific gravity of molybdenum, Michel once told me, is 95.5 – one of the heaviest metals, less heavy though than uranium, tungsten or lead. Legless, he weighs fifty-nine kilos. The colour alone of the stumps is like molybdenum, for they, unlike that monstrous metal, are alive. I know with my fingertips where their tissue is sensitive and the nerves murmur, and where the scarred flesh is numb, giving off warmth and taking in no sensation. On his back are light scars where they took skin to graft onto his face. Perhaps you are kissing my arse! he joked once when I was licking by his ear.

Without his artificial legs he hops like a bird on crutches. There are evenings when he lets me serve him like a king. Other times he is irritable and glowering and he pushes me away and, seizing his crutches, hops round the room like a plucked turkey. If he hears footsteps, when he's doing this, he flings himself onto the bed and pulls the sheet up to his grey beard. He has never let his daughter see him unharnessed. Passionately he wants his daughter to have an unmutilated father.

The wind is ruffling the sheet and the sheet is slapping like the washing in the orchard of my childhood when the bise blew. It won't blow away, Christian, are you sure?

Christian

come, he simply replied: Are you ready?

Strange how I'm not cold. I can feel each toe and each finger, they're warm as they were when I was a baby – I suddenly remember.

You take a man right into you and you cannot compare him or measure him or make a story of him. Everything that has ever been is swelling with the lips of the mouth into which you take him and he fills you, where you know as little as you know about an unborn child in your womb.

You can tell yourself other things about him when he has left, yet all of it remains far away compared to the places within you to which you lead him. Hay in the barn cannot change back into grass. If he's burning, the places to which you have led him are flooded with light. In your belly there are stars and of these stars you may be a victim. Poor Clotilde gave birth in the stable all alone, the door locked on the outside by her father.

It is painful for us to judge the man we have taken, for he's ours, already like a son. How can you judge a body which has been where he has been, who has come from there? Beside his single name all else is dead coals. How reluctant we are to judge! If we have to, if we are forced to, if we are picked up by the ears like a rabbit, we judge him and suffer the pain, the violence done to the sky within us where the stars shone. Men, poor men, judge more easily.

I never judged the life Stepan led before the Ram's Run. All that happened before the 31st of December 1953 was beyond judgement or comparison, for it had brought him to me in shed A, IN EUROPA. Since his disappearance, he has stayed with me where I first took him and hid him, beyond ashes. He has stayed with me as the seasons stay with the world.

The furnaces which robbed Stepan of his life took away from Michel his legs and now they are taking away his hearing. At night when he unfastens the prostheses he is

117

I will tell you which men deserve our respect. Men who give themselves to hard labour so that those close to them can eat. Men who are generous with everything they own. And men who spend their lives looking for God. The rest are pigshit.

Men aren't beautiful. Nothing has to stay in them. Nothing has to be attracted by any peace they offer. So they're not beautiful. Men have been given another power. They burn. They give off light and warmth. Sometimes they turn night into day. Often they destroy everything. Ashes are men's stuff. Milk is ours.

Once you've learnt to judge for yourself and are no more fooled by their boasts, it's not hard to tell the man who deserves respect and the man who is pigshit. Yet the power of a man to burn, we discover only by loving him. Does our love release the power? Not always. I loved Stepan for many weeks before we lived IN EUROPA. He was burning when I met him on the footbridge.

Michel I started to love when we returned to the village. We never got to Paris. I can die happily without seeing the capital. We stayed for three nights at the mad hotel with the white geese and his room opposite the wardrobes. Then we came home.

Once in the factory Stepan and Michel worked on the same shift for three days, yet it's in me they still meet. Marie-Noelle, Christian – embrace each other tonight, whatever happens, do this tonight, and know your fathers are embracing each other.

It is getting late and the light is already turning. The snow on the Gruvaz, facing west, is turning pink, the colour of the best rhubarb when cooked. I imagined we would come down to earth before it's dark, but Christian must know what he's doing. He's a national instructor, he came second in the European Championship of Hang-gliding and when I said to him, they've both gone to Annecy, they needn't know anything, need they? they won't be frightened, take me up this afternoon, the time's

116

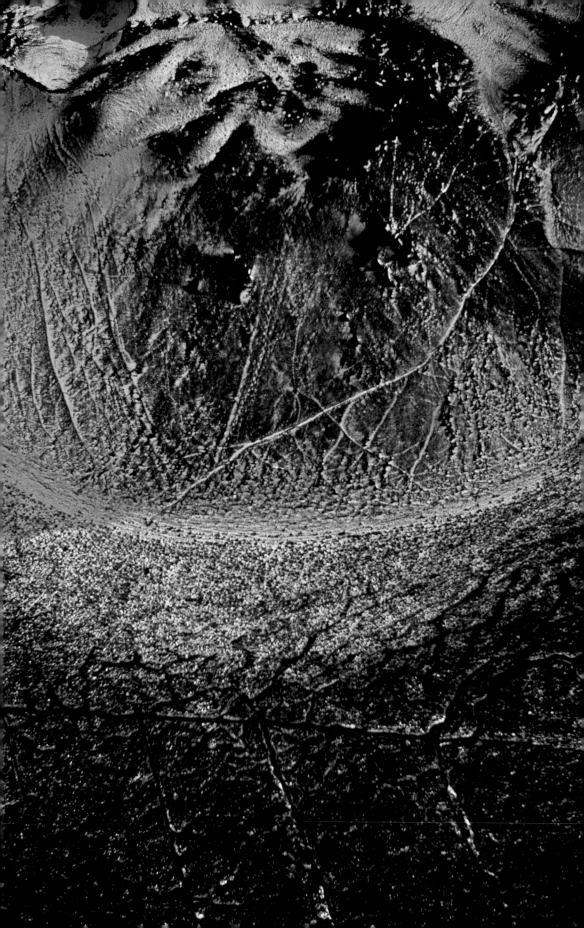